ROTHERHAM LIBRARY & INFORMATION SERVICES

This book must be returned by the date specified at the time
of issue as the Date Due for Return.
The loan may be extended (personally, by post or telephone)
for a further period, if the book is not required by another
reader, by quoting the above number.

LM1(C)

Other books by Nina Bawden

CARRIE'S WAR
THE FINDING
A HANDFUL OF THIEVES
HUMBUG
KEEPING HENRY
KEPT IN THE DARK
ON THE RUN
THE OUTSIDE CHILD
THE PEPPERMINT PIG
THE REAL PLATO JONES
REBEL ON A ROCK
THE ROBBERS
THE RUNAWAY SUMMER
THE SECRET PASSAGE
SQUIB
THE WHITE HORSE GANG

NINA BAWDEN

THE WITCH'S DAUGHTER

PUFFIN BOOKS

PUFFIN BOOKS

Published by the Penguin Group
Penguin Books Ltd, 27 Wrights Lane, London W8 5TZ, England
Penguin Books USA Inc., 375 Hudson Street, New York, New York 10014, USA
Penguin Books Australia Ltd, Ringwood, Victoria, Australia
Penguin Books Canada Ltd, 10 Alcorn Avenue, Toronto, Ontario, Canada M4V 3B2
Penguin Books (NZ) Ltd, 182–190 Wairau Road, Auckland 10, New Zealand

Penguin Books Ltd, Registered Offices: Harmondsworth, Middlesex, England

First published by Victor Gollancz 1966
Published in Puffin Books 1969
25 27 29 30 28 26 24

Copyright © Nina Bawden, 1966
All rights reserved

Printed in England by Clays Ltd, St Ives plc
Set in Monotype Bembo

CONTENTS

1 Bewitched 7

2 A Piece of Glass Worth a King's Ransom 18

3 Carlin's Cave 29

4 Mr Hoggart has an Accident 40

5 There was Someone Else in the Room 48

6 The Girl on the Beach 55

7 What is a Diamond? 65

8 Wrecked Ships and Treasure 74

9 The Heroic Behaviour of Mr Jones 79

10 Unexpected Evidence 86

11 Abandoned 96

12 A Kind of Magic 104

13 A Little Wild Thing, Half-Crazed 114

14 Golf Clubs and Lobsters 125

15 On the Rocks 132

16 A Needle in a Haystack 139

17 A Bunch of Flowers for Janey 151

For Perdita and Kate

I

BEWITCHED

THE witch's daughter sat on a rock in the bay. It was a huge rock, with steep sides of black basalt, turreted like a castle and crowned with purple heather. On one side the sea thundered, throwing up spray like white lace. Inland, the wet sand of low tide stretched back to the dunes and the brown slopes of Ben Luin beyond. The bay was empty except for a few bullocks at the water's edge and the gulls that swooped and cried like kittens over the shore and the hills of this Scottish island of Skua. The witch's daughter closed her eyes and flew with the gulls in the air: she turned and dived and felt the wind cold on her face. She flew in her mind: her body sat still on the rock. Her name was Perdita, which means lost.

Her eyelids fluttered open. She looked out to sea and saw the red steamer from the mainland moving across the bay. Perdita stood up and turned inland. Once off the heathery cap of the rock, the way down was dangerous, but she was neat and unhesitating as a deer. Her feet were bare, her boots tied round her neck with string. She wore a woman's dress, cut down but still too long for her, and a green scarf round her hair. The bullocks watched her with their black-lashed, mild eyes as she ran across the sand. She vanished among the spiky grass of the dunes and then reappeared, climbing upwards across a patch of cropped turf to a dry-stone wall. Over the wall, she stopped to put on her boots. The peat bog squelched beneath her, tugging at her boots, but she trudged sturdily on, working her way round the side of Ben Luin towards one of its lower ridges. When she reached the top of this ridge, she paused for breath and looked down at the town of Skuaphort, a small cluster of white houses round a harbour and a stone jetty. Small boats

7

rocked at anchor on the land side of the jetty and, out in deeper water, the steamer was slowly rounding the point and coming into harbour.

Perdita ran down the stony side of the crag, scattering sheep and starting up a hare that loped a little way before it froze still, pretending to be invisible. She reached the stone road by the ruined cottage and jumped the stream, because the little bridge that had once crossed it, when the cottage was lived in, was ruined too. Once on the road, she went slower because the stones were loose and would roll under her feet if she were careless. The town was farther than it looked. By the time she reached the harbour, the steamer was already tied up, and beginning to unload.

There were other children tumbling out of the white houses and racing towards the jetty. The witch's daughter avoided them, hiding behind an angle of the school-house wall until they had gone safely past her. Hugging the walls of the build-ings, she kept her eyes on the ground as if she did not want to see, or be seen. She hopped off the road on to the shore and made her way over the rocks that were slippery with gingery seaweed, to a beached boat. She crouched behind the boat, to watch.

Besides the half dozen children, there were men on the jetty: John McAllister the postman, waiting with the mail van; Will Campbell with his box of lobsters for Oban; Mr Duncan from the shop, to fetch his supplies. These were being carried off now, down the swaying gangplank: crates of groceries, grey containers of Calor Gas. Perdita waited. She was not interested in Mr Duncan's supplies. She was interested in people. New people. Was anyone going to land? It was not very likely, she knew – more people left Skua than ever came to it now – but all the same, she craned hopefully from the shelter of the boat, her eyes fixed on the steamer. Then she gave a little sigh of satisfaction. Four people had appeared on deck, a man, a woman and two children: a fair-haired boy and a younger girl.

The boy ran down off the boat but the girl, who had come with him to the head of the gangplank, hung back, waiting. As Perdita watched, the woman joined her and placed one of the girl's hands on the rail. She said something and the child lifted her foot to place it on the gangplank, lifting it rather higher than was necessary. Then, with the woman guiding her, she came hesitantly down, seeming to feel the way with her feet, until she stood on the jetty. The woman left her there and returned to the deck to help the man carry suitcases off the steamer.

The girl had long, brown hair that blew in the wind. She put up a hand to hold back her hair and looked out from the jetty. Perdita thought she was looking straight at her.

Perdita looked round. No one else had noticed her. Cautiously, she came out from behind the boat and scrambled over the rocks towards the jetty until she was standing beneath it, out of sight of the other people, but in full view of the girl. She was about her own age, Perdita thought, which was ten years seven months old. Perdita looked at her and then smiled shyly. The girl did not smile back, but bent her head sideways, as if listening. Puzzled, because she did not seem unfriendly or nervous of her, like the island children, Perdita stopped smiling. The girl took one tentative step towards the edge of the jetty, and then another . . .

'Janey. *Janey* . . .' The woman's voice was sharp, as if she were alarmed. She came up beside the girl. 'You're rather near the edge, my darling,' she said, and took her hand.

The girl, Janey, stiffened impatiently, humping one shoulder higher than the other in a fretful gesture. 'Don't *shout*, Mummy,' she said. 'How can I see if you shout?'

Perdita thought this a strange thing to say. With the aid of a chain, she hoisted herself up over the edge of the jetty. Her head and shoulders were in full view now, but she was suddenly too curious about this odd girl to be afraid someone might see her, and, indeed, for a little while she was safe enough:

the weekly steamer was an event on Skua and absorbed every-one's attention.

Clinging to the chain, she watched the newcomers being greeted by Mr Tarbutt, who kept the small hotel, the only hotel on Skua. He had put on his best suit for the occasion and was beaming all over his round face, which shone rosily, like a varnished apple. Since his hotel was often empty, even in the short, summer season, this was a red letter day for him: besides the family of four, there was another visitor, a fat man with short legs who carried a long, canvas bag with knobs sticking out one end. Since Perdita had never seen golf clubs, she did not recognize them. Mr Tarbutt had a trolley for the luggage and was loading suitcases on to it. The fair-haired boy was helping him. He was very eager and excited and talked all the time, but in such a quick English voice, that Perdita could not understand what he said. His sister, Janey, said and did nothing. She stood quite still while her mother talked to Mr Tarbutt. When her father came off the boat, carrying the last of the suit-cases, he set them down by the trolley and put his hand on her shoulder. 'Here we are, then. Think you're going to like it, darling?'

Janey shook back her long brown hair. 'It smells like a lovely place,' she said, and, suddenly, Perdita understood why she had not smiled back at her before. Understanding, she pursed her lips to make a soft, warbling cry, like a sleepy bird. Janey turned. Perdita warbled again, so low that only someone listen-ing really hard could have heard her, and this time Janey did smile back, a quick, delighted, friendly smile, before her father led her away to follow the trolley which was loaded now and being pulled by Mr Tarbutt, off the jetty and up the one stony street of Skuaphort, towards the hotel.

Perdita watched her go, too interested to remember that now the bustle of the steamer landing was over, one of the island children would be bound to notice her.

As, of course, one of them did. Alistair Campbell, who

had been helping his father bring down the lobsters, nudged the boy next to him. In the space of perhaps thirty seconds, all the children on the jetty fell silent. Perdita became conscious of the fixed gaze of six pairs of eyes. Her enemies were standing in a semi-circle, watching her.

At once, she ducked down, slipping her hand over the chain and grazing the palm. She made her way over the rocks towards the road. The children ran off the jetty and round the harbour after her. They could have caught her up quite easily, since she had to go slowly over the slippery rocks, but they seemed to prefer to keep their distance. Once she was on the road and trudging uphill, out of the town, they followed her in a giggling group, stopping when she glanced back over her shoulder but moving on as soon as she turned round again, as if playing a game of Grandmother's Footsteps. Perdita lifted her chin and faced stubbornly into the wind. She intended to ignore them. She would have ignored them, if Alistair Campbell had not thrown a stone. It was a small stone, no more than a pebble, and he threw it half-heartedly, so that it did no harm, only clattered on the ground behind Perdita's heels, but it made her angry. She wheeled round to face them, her face set and fierce, her eyes glinting like chips of green glass. The island children stood still. For a long minute, none of them moved or spoke: they stood as if spellbound. Then one of the younger ones sniggered nervously, the sound cut off short as his big sister clapped her hand over his mouth, and Alistair Campbell, the oldest of them all, plucked up his courage and turned to run. They all gasped and followed him, stones scudding under their feet. The little boy who had sniggered slipped and fell, but his sister jerked him to his feet before he had time to wail and dragged him after her, looking fearfully over her shoulder.

Perdita watched them until they disappeared behind the school house. Her eyes were no longer angry. She was not frightened of them. They were frightened of her, and that was worse: a sad and lonely thing to know. She sighed a little and rubbed the back of her hand across her eyes, as if they were itching. Then she turned back to the road and began the long trudge home.

Home was a white house on the shore of an inland loch. The house was called Luinpool. There was a stone wall round it and a few trees, bent and flattened on the top with wind. There were no other houses and no other trees within sight, only the loch and the bare hills. There had once been a garden round the house but all that was left of it now was a line of the green glass balls that are used as floats for lobster pots, edging the path, and an old, wild fuchsia bush by the front door.

The front door did not open. Years of damp and disuse had jammed it solid. Perdita went in by the back door straight into the big, dark kitchen. The last of the day's light filtered through a small window, but it was pale beside the leaping, yellow glow of the fire in the range oven. Annie MacLaren was bending over the fire, riddling the ashes.

'Late,' she scolded, reaching up for the polished brass rail above the fire and pulling herself upright. She was rheumaticky and old; her grey hair so thin that her pink scalp showed through.

Perdita said nothing. She sat on the settle, pulled off her boots and set them in the hearth to dry.

'Porridge on the stove,' Annie MacLaren said, and went to the table to trim the oil lamp.

'Don't light the lamp yet. It's nice, just the fire,' Perdita said.

Annie MacLaren hesitated. Then she turned to the fire and ladled porridge out of a black pot into a bowl. She took a spoon from the dresser. 'There you are, lady.'

She sat in a sagging chair opposite Perdita and watched her eat. Her knobbly old hands were folded in her lap. The kettle murmured on the hob, droplets of water from its spout hissed into the fire. An unseen clock ticked in a dark corner of the room. There was wind in the chimney.

Perdita wriggled her cold feet deep into the rag rug and finished her porridge. 'There's new people come today,' she said. 'Two men and a woman and a boy. And a girl, who is blind.'

'You've not been down to the harbour?'

Perdita shook her head.

Annie MacLaren's voice was troubled. 'You know what *he* said. I promised him.'

'I've not been.' Perdita stared into the fire. There was a little puff of gas, burning green.

'You must have talked to someone, then. Else how would you know?'

'About the new people?' Perdita closed her eyes and smiled secretly. 'I can see through walls and round corners,' she said in a sing-song chant. 'I can fly over the mountains and over the sea. I know who comes and who goes, and they never see me.'

Annie MacLaren gave an uneasy laugh. 'Maybe he'll not believe that, lady.'

Perdita peeped at Annie slyly, through lowered lashes. 'You believe it though . . .'

Annie MacLaren stirred in her chair and the old springs creaked. 'Well, you've got Powers,' she said, half grudging, half respectful. 'Though to my mind, seeing through walls is one thing, flying's another . . .' A piece of coal fell through the bars and blackened slowly on the hearth. Annie creaked forward to push it under the grate and sank back in her chair with a grunt. 'I know what I know, I'll not deny it. But *he* thinks it – well – fanciful. So you'd better keep quiet, lady. Don't go chattering to him about new people off the steamer. He might think you've been down to the town, mixing and talking. He doesn't want talk. I promised him there wouldn't be any.'

Perdita sat hunched on the settle. 'I don't see why I shouldn't go where I want. I'm not afraid of Mr Smith.'

'No one's asking you to be. Just quiet and respectful and

13

doing what he says. Don't mix, don't talk. Then there'll be no trouble.' Annie MacLaren paused, and then mumbled, half to herself. 'I don't want trouble. Just a bit of peace and comfort in my old age.' She leaned her head against the high back of the the chair, and closed her eyes. She fell asleep very quickly, as old people do. Her mouth drooped open.

Chin on hand, the little girl watched the fire. The clock ticked, the kettle hissed, the coals settled in the grate. Suddenly, Perdita straightened up, listening. She jumped off the settle and tugged at Annie MacLaren's skirt to waken her. 'Mr Smith's come,' she said loudly. 'Light the lamps, I'll open the gate.'

She ran out into the yard, disturbing a sleepy hen who had chosen to roost on the pile of peat by the back door. The wind snatched her skirt and blew it up full, like a sail. She stumbled up the rutted track to the gate and opened it to let in a white Jaguar car that purred into the yard, bumping over the ruts, and stopped in front of the back door. Perdita swung on the gate to close it, and ran back to the house.

Mr Smith was getting out of the car. He was medium height, neither thin nor fat, neither young nor old. He wore dark glasses and carried a wooden box under his arm. 'How's my favourite witch?' he said, not smiling, but friendly. He touched Perdita on the cheek and they went together into the kitchen.

Annie MacLaren had lit two oil lamps. She gave one to Mr Smith. 'Fire's alight, I'll get your tea,' she said.

He put the wooden box he was carrying down on the table, and took the lamp. 'A word with you, Annie,' he said, and went out of the kitchen into the dark hall beyond. Annie MacLaren followed him. They were away about five minutes. When the old woman came back, she looked harassed. 'He's got a visitor tonight. He wants lobsters cooked. You'd better get to bed. Out of the way.'

'Can't I help, Annie?'

She shook her head. 'His friend won't like it. He may know you're here, but he won't want to see you. Out of sight, out of mind.'

Perdita opened her mouth and closed it. When Annie MacLaren was firm, which wasn't often, it was no use pleading. 'I'll get in some coal, then,' she said.

Outside, it was a wild night, but clear. Above the raggedy clouds, there was a moon sailing. The coal heap glistened in the light. Perdita filled the bucket and staggered back to the house.

'Too full. You'll strain yourself,' Annie MacLaren grumbled.

Perdita set the bucket down and rubbed her arm. 'I'm strong, stronger than you, Annie. Can I see the lobsters?'

There were two in the box, wet and black. They stirred slightly, making a whispering sound.

'Will Campbell sent lobsters to Oban today,' Perdita said. 'Did Mr Smith go fishing with Will Campbell?'

'I daresay. He goes sometimes.'

'Why does he? He never eats lobsters. Why does he catch them if he doesn't like to eat them?'

'Sport, maybe. Or to send to his friends.'

'Mr Smith doesn't have any friends. No one comes . . .'

'Someone's coming tonight. And he's partial to lobsters, Mr Smith says. Get your candle now,' Annie MacLaren said.

Perdita fetched her candle from the mantelpiece where it stood beside the orange and white china dog. The hot water tank beside the range fire was clicking. 'He's having a bath,' Perdita said hopefully. 'Will I lay the table in his room, Annie?'

'No. Off to bed.'

The candle flame danced in the draught as Perdita left the kitchen and went into the high, dark hall. The ceiling disappeared in shadow, her own shadow walked beside her, up the stairs. The house was big: it had once been a manse where the minister had lived, but that was a long time ago. When Mr Smith came to Skua, it had stood empty for years: there was no land with it, and, even if there had been, no one would have wanted such a great old place with the plaster falling from the walls and the roof sagging in places. No one, except Mr Smith. He had put in a bathroom and repaired two rooms for himself: otherwise, though he had been there three years, he had done nothing. There were attic rooms where the rain came through and some rooms that were shut up altogether, empty except for mice and dust and the wind that came through the floor boards and the rattling window frames, so that the house seemed, in spite of its emptiness, to be always alive and breathing.

It might have seemed, to most people, a strange, lonely sort of place, unsuitable for a little girl to grow up in. Certainly Mr Smith had thought so. 'It's no place for a child,' he had said, when he had engaged Annie MacLaren as his housekeeper, just after he came to the island. 'You must leave her with someone. A relation. Surely she must have some relation.'

'She has no one but me,' Annie MacLaren had said. 'I'll see she's not in your way.'

Mr Smith had frowned. 'I've had – business worries. I must have peace and quiet. A child is out of the question.'

'I'll keep her quiet,' Annie MacLaren had said flatly. Her old face, stony and stubborn, showed none of the despair she was feeling. Until a few months back, she and her brother had farmed a small croft. The brother had died and she had had to sell the croft for a pathetically small sum which was now almost gone: she was desperate for this chance to keep body and soul together.

'I must have absolute privacy. *Absolute*. Whatever goes on in this house, whoever comes – not a word must get out.' He looked carefully at Annie MacLaren. 'Do you find that strange?'

'A man has a right to mind his own business,' Annie Mac-Laren had said.

'Not an easy thing to do, with a child in the house.'

'She's only little.'

'She'll grow. Chatter to other children, carry tales . . .'

'Not this one.' Annie MacLaren had been nervous of the effect her insistence might have, because if she lost this job, what would she do, where would she go? But she had insisted just the same. 'The others won't play with her.' She had hesitated, wondering how much this city-bred man from England would understand. 'They say she's bewitched,' she had said finally. 'A witch's daughter.'

'Bewitched?' Mr Smith's eyes were hidden behind his dark glasses, but his lips smiled. 'Bewitched?' he repeated, and suddenly burst out laughing. 'What on earth do you mean?'

But because he had laughed, Annie MacLaren was deeply offended and refused to tell him, even when he said, on a wave of good humour, that it was all right, she could bring the child if she wanted, not even much later, when they were all settled at Luinpool and he would play with Perdita, when he was in a good mood, calling her his little changeling, his little witch . . .

Now, three years later, he still thought it an excellent joke.

2

A PIECE OF GLASS WORTH A KING'S RANSOM

THE moon, falling full on her face, woke Perdita up. She slipped from her bed to look out of the window. The clouds were hanging in a long, black ridge over Ben Luin and the moon was drifting in a clear sky. The air was almost still: the wind pump was still creaking, but only slowly, and the surface of the loch was silvery calm.

Perdita felt sticky from sleep. She would have liked to open the window but the sash was jammed tight with wooden wedges because Annie MacLaren believed the night air was dangerous to health. As a result, Perdita's tiny bedroom, which was only just large enough to hold a small bed and a chair, was airless and hot, so hot that she felt she could not bear it a moment longer. It looked cool and peaceful outside. She took her dress from the hook on the back of the door and slipped it on over her nightdress which, like her dress, was one of Annie MacLaren's cut down.

She opened her door. Across the landing, Annie MacLaren's door was open, but Perdita knew she was safely asleep because she could hear the old woman muttering and creaking the bed springs: when she was asleep, she lay still. Barefoot, Perdita slipped past her door and down the stairs. At the bottom, she looked along the hall and saw a light under Mr Smith's door. She heard him laugh and crept closer, to listen.

'Golf clubs,' he said, 'Golf clubs! For a holiday on Skua! What d'you think this place is, man? A holiday camp?'

A strange voice answered, sounding injured. 'How was I to know? Scottish island, *you* said. Well, they play a lot of golf in

Scotland, *I* thought. So I bought a set of clubs. Sort of disguise, like. Cost me a packet, I don't mind telling you.'

'Disguise? You might as well have worn a thumping great wig. Or a false nose. It wouldn't have been any more noticeable. Golf clubs!' Mr Smith snorted. 'A good laugh like that will be right round the island by morning.'

Perdita thought he sounded in a good-humoured, teasing mood. At the same time, she realized she was hungry. A bowl of porridge was not very much to go to bed on. It filled you up at the time, but left you empty later. And Annie MacLaren was safely asleep. She would never know Perdita had disobeyed her.

She opened the door a crack. The oil lamp was turned low: most of the light came from the peat fire, which, in spite of the warm night, was banked up high. Two men sat on either side of it: Mr Smith and the short, fat man she had seen on the jetty this morning. Between them was a small table with two glasses and a bottle of whisky on it: on another, larger table, that stood between Perdita and the fire, the remains of a good meal. She saw bread, cheese, butter – and felt her stomach groan with emptiness. Holding her breath, she slipped just inside the room.

'You didn't, by any chance, ask where the golf club was?' Mr Smith was asking, politely.

'Well – as a matter of fact – oh, all right, I *did*. Mr Tarbutt just said there wasn't one.'

Mr Smith reached for his glass and drained it. 'He didn't laugh in your face? No – he wouldn't do that. Too polite. But it'll make talk, *that*'s the pity. Still, maybe it'll be all right. Maybe they'll just think you're a bit cracked. As long as they don't connect ...' Mr Smith drew in his breath and leaned forward. 'No one saw you come here?'

The stranger shook his head. 'I did what you said. Said I was tired, went to bed. Then got out of the window. And walked. Three miles, you said.' He gave a short laugh. 'Seemed more like thirty. Oh, my poor feet.' There was a crackle as he took a bag of sweets out of his pocket, unwrapped what looked like a toffee, and popped it into his mouth.

'Island miles,' Mr Smith explained. 'Different from what you're used to, like every other kind of measure. Time, for instance. Tomorrow doesn't mean what you think – not here. It means next week, next month – even next year. You ought to live here a while, you'd find out!' He spoke distinctly and bitterly, as if he wasn't, Perdita thought, in such a good mood after all. That was a pity, but she was so hungry – surely, whatever mood he was in, he wouldn't be angry if she said she was hungry? Moving silently on her bare feet, she stole nearer to the table.

'Oh, look here,' the stranger said. 'It don't seem to me you've got much to complain of. Place is pretty as a picture. Mountains, sheep. Communing with Nature. Romantic, that's what it is!'

'I'd like to see you communing with Nature,' Mr Smith said. The stranger chuckled. 'Maybe you're right. I like to see a bit of life. Still, at least you're fixed up cosy enough.' A faint acrimony entered his voice. 'I haven't had it so easy. Sweating out a nine to five job, knowing there was no need. Waiting . . .'

'D'you think it's been easy waiting here?' Mr Smith leaned forward to pour himself a generous helping of whisky. 'Stuck in this dead and alive hole for three years? There've been times when I thought I'd go mad. Nothing to do, no one to talk to – no one but an ignorant old woman and . . .'

A shout from the other man stopped him short. 'Good God, what's *this* . . .'

Full face, he looked rather like a frog, with a broad, flat mouth and bulgy eyes, set high in a bald forehead. Those eyes stared at Perdita in a way that made her tremble. She slipped round the table for safety and got behind Mr Smith's chair. He reached out a long arm and pulled her round to face him. *His* eyes were hidden behind his glasses, but his mouth was angry. 'What are you up to? I thought I told Annie . . .'

''Twasn't her fault,' Perdita pleaded. 'She told me not to. Only I woke up and I was so hungry.'

'How long have you been here?' Frog Face shouted. He jumped to his feet and stood on the hearth, short, fat legs planted solid as trees. 'Spying – I'll teach you to spy . . .'

Mr Smith said quickly, 'There's no need to speak to the child like that.'

'Wants a whipping,' Frog Face said. 'A good whipping. And if she was anything to do with me, that's what she'd get. Spying on a private conversation.'

'She means no harm,' Mr Smith said. 'Tells no tales, either. Not if she's treated properly.' He spoke in a meaning voice, and Frog Face swallowed hard. He looked at Mr Smith and then sat down in his chair, seeming to collapse suddenly, like a balloon when the air is let out of it. He took a red silk handkerchief out of his breast pocket, mopped his bald forehead, and smiled at Perdita. It was a damp, forced smile. 'Sorry,' he said, 'weakness of mine. Always lose my temper when taken by surprise.'

Perdita was not taken in by the smile: the expression in his eyes remained the same as before. As if conscious of this, he smiled more broadly, to compensate. 'So you didn't mean to be a naughty spy, then? You're a good little girl, are you? Are you a little girl who can keep secrets, I wonder?'

'She doesn't carry tales,' Mr Smith said. 'I told you.'

Frog Face looked at him. 'You never said there was a kid. Taking a chance, weren't you?'

'Not so much as might appear,' Mr Smith said. 'And anyway, chances have to be taken. You took a chance on me, didn't you?'

Still looking at him, Frog Face nodded, slowly. 'I reckon I did,' he said. He smiled again, more naturally this time, and settled back in his chair. 'After the shock, a spot of liquid refreshment wouldn't come amiss,' he remarked, unwrapped another toffee, and put it in his mouth.

Mr Smith poured whisky. 'Take the glass over to the gentle-man, Perdita,' he said, 'and introduce yourself. This is Mr Jones. Mr Jones,' he repeated, smiling to himself suddenly, as if Mr Jones's name was an exceedingly funny joke.

Hesitantly, Perdita did as she was told. Mr Jones took the whisky with one hand, with the other he caught Perdita's wrist and drew her close to his fat knee.

'Perdita,' he said, mumbling his toffee, 'that's pretty. Un-usual, too. How old are you, Perdita?'

'Ten. Going on eleven,' Perdita said, disliking the feel of his clammy hand on her wrist, but not daring to pull away.

Mr Jones looked surprised. 'You don't look that old to me. I've got two girls. One nine, one ten. The nine year old is a good bit bigger than you.'

'She's small for her age,' Mr Smith said.

'Small? Skinny, I'd say. Looks underfed to me,' Mr Jones answered.

He lifted his glass and took a long swallow. His Adam's apple wobbled up and down. He set his empty glass down on the table and nodded solemnly while Mr Smith re-filled it. 'Kids need a lot of nourishment, you know, Smithie. Milk. Vitamins. Orange juice. My word – it's quite an expense, feeding a child.' He picked up his whisky glass and cradled it lovingly to his chest. 'Expense and worry. Worry and expense. That's what children mean. I was saying to the wife, only the other day . . .'

Mr Smith interrupted him. 'Are you hungry?' he asked Perdita.

She turned, slipping her hand gently out of Frog Face's grasp. Now she had stopped being frightened, she had begun to notice her empty stomach again.

'You'd better have something to eat, then.' Mr Smith stood up and went over to the table. 'There's lobster left. Would you like that? And a glass of wine?'

'Poison to a child,' Mr Jones said loudly from his chair. 'Milk, Smithie, milk. That's what she needs. Good, fresh milk.

22

And no lobster. *Positively* no lobster. Unsuitable for a young stomach.'

'Cheese?' Mr Smith asked tentatively. Frog Face seemed to have fallen into a doze and he raised his voice. 'Come on – tell me what to give her. You're the family man.'

Frog Face blew out through his lips. 'Cheese in moderation. Not at night, though. It lies heavy.'

Mr Smith sighed. 'There doesn't seem much else. What does Annie give you, Perdita?'

'Porridge,' Perdita said. 'Potatoes. And bits of other things. What you leave over.' Annie MacLaren had told her that Mr Smith had been good to them and it would be wrong to repay him by eating him out of house and home.

Frog Face laughed from his chair. 'Keeping the servants short, eh? Shame on you, Smithie . . .'

Mr Smith looked worried. 'I've never had anything to do with children. I'd have thought the old woman would have had more sense . . .' He cut a good piece of cheese and several slices of bread, buttering them thickly. Then he wiped out a used glass with his handkerchief and filled it to the brim with creamy milk.

'She won't come to much harm if she gets outside of that,' Frog Face said.

Perdita sat on a stool by the fire. While she ate, the two men watched her, not talking, and after a while the silence and the food and the warmth from the fire made her feel sleepy. Her eyelids drooped, her stomach felt tight as a drum. She leaned back against the arm of Mr Smith's chair and dozed . . .

While she slept, someone must have lifted her and placed her in a chair. The next thing she knew was the roughness of the chair cover under her cheek, and the murmuring sound of voices.

'. . . thinking of South America,' Mr Jones was saying. 'But the wife isn't keen, not at all. Doesn't want to interrupt the girls' education, she says. Very keen on their schooling. There'll be schools in South America, I tell her, but she says it won't be the same. She wants to stay put, that's the truth of it . . .'

'Sensible woman,' Mr Smith said, rather dryly. 'It's what I told you to do, wasn't it? Stay put, sit tight. Enjoy a bit of extra comfort here and there . . .'

'Not enough, Smithie . . .' Suddenly Mr Jones's voice was pleading. 'Come on, be fair. Put yourself in my place. Would it have been enough for you, knowing what you'd got in that box there? Lap of luxury all your life, not just comfort. And *freedom* . . .' His voice sank, lingered lovingly. 'Freedom, Smithie . . .'

'Let's hope it turns out that way,' Mr Smith said.

Perdita yawned and stretched. There was a sudden, sharp sound as of a metal lid slamming shut. She sat up sleepily and saw the two men standing and looking at her. Frog Face put out one hand as if to cover up a small box on the table in front of him; then he seemed to think better of it, tucked both hands into his pockets and smiled at her benignly.

'Woke up, have you?' he said. He nodded at Mr Smith. 'Bed's the best place.'

Perdita slipped off the chair rubbing her eyes. One of her legs had gone to sleep, making her stagger, and Frog Face caught her arm to steady her.

'One thing first, though,' he said. 'Smithie here says you don't carry tales. I believe him, so you won't, will you? Not about me.' He shook her a little, in a friendly enough way, but there was a warning in his voice. 'Forget you ever saw me, eh?'

'She knows,' Mr Smith says. 'Don't you, witch?'

Perdita nodded.

'That's good.' Frog Face smiled fatly. 'You're a good little girl. Good little girls sometimes get nice presents.' He paused. 'What would you think was a nice present?'

'I don't know,' Perdita murmured.

'There's no need,' Mr Smith said sharply. 'The child's not used to presents.'

'Oh come,' Frog Face said. 'Little girls are the same the world over.' His voice was coaxing. 'There must be something she'd like, something she wants . . .'

Sleepiness had made Perdita bold. 'All I want,' she said suddenly, 'the *only* thing I want, is to go to school.'

'*School?*' Frog Face said, astonished. 'Don't you go to school?'

Mr Smith answered for her. 'No. She doesn't. Never has. I don't think she can even read and write.' He hesitated. 'She runs wild. Like a little wild cat.'

'Good heavens!' Frog Face said. 'But she can't – I mean, she can't not go to school. Good heavens, man, that's against the *law*.'

Perdita was awake enough, now, to wonder why Mr Smith should laugh so merrily at that.

'Not really,' he said, after a minute. 'There is a school at Skuaphort, but it's more than three miles and there's no bus to fetch her. And unless they fetch her, they can't insist. Not legally. So they turn a blind eye.'

Frog Face whistled through his teeth. 'I think that's terrible,' he said, very slowly and seriously. 'I don't know what the wife would say, I really don't. A child should go to school.'

Perdita looked at him. 'I want to go to school,' she said, 'and learn to read and write, and then, when I'm older, I want to go to the big school on Trull.' Frog Face was staring at her, and she thought perhaps he didn't know where Trull was, as he was a stranger. 'Trull's the big island,' she said, 'with an airport and a cinema and this fine, big school.' She stopped, her heart banging against her ribs. She had never said this to anyone before. It was strange – if she had had time to think, she would have thought it strange – that she should have said it to Frog Face whom she barely knew, and didn't, really, like very much.

Mr Smith was watching her. He said, to Frog Face, 'In the

circumstances, it's convenient she doesn't go, don't you think?' And then he gave her hair a little tug, to tease her, and added, 'It wouldn't do, not for a witch's daughter. If you mixed with other children, you'd lose your Powers. You'd grow ordinary like them.'

Perdita said, 'I wouldn't mind being ordinary if I could learn to read and write.'

Mr Jones was making a face as if he was sorry for her. Perdita thought he was the sort of person who could easily be terribly angry with you one minute, and very sorry for you the next. He said, pulling this long face, 'Poor kiddie. It's a shame, it really is . . .' His eyes were bright and shining, almost as if he were going to cry. 'Well, we'll have to think of something to make up for it, won't we?' he said, and suddenly his sad look was gone and he was grinning all over his face. 'Shut your eyes,' he said.

Perdita shut her eyes. There was a little click. She heard Mr Smith say, very softly, '*Don't*, you fool . . .' and Frog Face laughed, and said, 'Why not, after all? There's plenty more where that came from . . .' Then there was a rattling sound as if small stones – or sweets – were being tipped on to the table.

Behind her closed eyelids, Perdita tried to see what was going on. Often – not always, but often – if she kept quiet and concentrated hard, she could see what people were doing, even if her eyes were closed or she was on the other side of a wall, but tonight there had been so much talk to distract her, and she was very tired. . . . Although she tried as hard as she could, she could only guess. And, because Frog Face had been eating toffees, she guessed there were toffees in the tin, and that he was going to give her one.

The two men were muttering to each other, but so low that she couldn't hear what they were saying, until Mr Smith laughed. It was a high, queerly excited laugh. 'Hold out your hand, Perdita,' he said.

Obediently, she did so. Something hard and cold was placed in her open palm.

'Open your eyes now.' She opened her eyes. She was holding a small stone – only it was prettier than any stone she had ever seen on the beaches of Skua. It was transparent, like glass: when she turned it over, it caught the reflection from the fire and looked, for a minute, like a piece of fire itself.

She looked up at the two men.

'Do you like it?' Frog Face asked. 'Do you like your present?'

'It's very pretty, thank you,' Perdita said, though in fact she was rather disappointed: she would have preferred a toffee. And then, because Frog Face looked as if he were expecting her to say something more, she added, 'It's a very pretty piece of glass.'

Mr Smith turned away. He poured himself a glass of whisky with a hand that was not quite steady. Frog Face made a small, yelping sound. 'Piece of glass worth a king's ransom,' he said, wiping his eyes with his handkerchief. His face was red and laughing.

Mr Smith was laughing too, so much that some of the whisky slopped out of his glass and spilled down his waistcoat.

'What shall I do with it?' Perdita asked him.

'Wear it round your neck on a piece of string,' he said, and exploded in another burst of laughter.

Frog Face answered her more seriously. 'Keep it safe, it'll bring you luck,' he said. Then he hesitated before adding, 'But only if you keep it safe, mind. Don't go showing it to anyone.'

Perdita shook her head a little impatiently. Annie MacLaren would not be interested in a piece of old glass, any more than she was in the shells Perdita collected on the beach. And who else was there, to show it to?

Mr Smith had stopped laughing. He said, to the other man, 'You'd best take your own advice. Don't go blabbing. Or drinking, down at the town. It loosens the tongue.'

'What d'you take me for?' Frog Face asked indignantly.

Mr Smith did not answer him. Instead, he said to Perdita, 'Off to bed, now. Take your present and get off to bed.'

He spoke, not unkindly but brusquely, as if he had suddenly grown tired of some game they were playing. This was a way he had: he would play with her, idly amusing himself, but the instant he tired he would dismiss her without warning, turning her summarily out of the room as if she were a tiresome puppy or a kitten. Since Perdita was used to it, she did not resent his behaviour. She went now without a word, out of the room and up the dark stairs.

She got into bed and lay there, sleepily fingering her stone and wondering if it really was lucky, as Frog Face had said, and how long he would stay, and where South America was, and if it was an island like Skua, or a big country like Scotland. Yawning, she listened to the men's voices murmuring on downstairs. Just as she was drifting off to sleep, they must have opened the door and come into the hall, because she heard Frog Face say quite clearly, 'No – no one else staying at the hotel. Only this man Hoggart and his wife and a couple of kids. He's a botanist – funny sort of occupation for a grown man, collecting flowers!'

Mr Smith said something she couldn't catch and then Frog Face laughed. 'Don't worry yourself, Smithie. I don't suppose they've even noticed me.'

3

CARLIN'S CAVE

'He must be absolutely barmy,' Timothy Hoggart said. 'Crazy as a coot.'

'Who?' his father asked, without much interest. He was pre-occupied with easing Mr Tarbutt's old Ford over a deep rut in the rough road.

'That chap.'

'What chap?'

Tim sighed heavily. 'It's amazing, the way you don't notice people. The man with the golf clubs who eats toffees all the time.'

'Oh, *that* man. Jones, his name is. Open the gate, Tim.'

Tim got out. The gate was tied up with wire in an extremely complicated system of knots that took a long time to undo. Once he had opened the gate, and the old car had jolted through, it took almost as long to tie the gate up again. 'It's awfully inefficient,' Tim complained when he got back into the car. 'All these gates. I mean, I know they've got to have gates because of the animals, but they might make them a bit easier to open. It's such a waste of time.'

'There's plenty of time on Skua. You might say it's about the only thing there *is* plenty of, so people can afford to waste it.' Mr Hoggart laughed to himself, pushing his glasses up on his nose. 'At least there's a gate to open. There's a place I know in Ireland where they simply build the wall across the road: when a car wants to go through, they knock the wall down and build it up again.'

Tim's mouth gaped open. Then, through the front window of the car, he saw something that made him shriek with delight. 'Dad – look – an eagle . . .'

Mr Hoggart put on the brakes, banging Tim's nose against the windscreen. 'Glasses, Tim.'

Tim grabbed the field glasses from the glove compartment and gave them to his father. After a minute, Mr Hoggart gave a disappointed sigh. 'Only a buzzard. As a matter of fact, I don't think there are any eagles on Skua. There he goes . . .'

They watched as the big, brown bird sailed slowly overhead and disappeared between two peaks of the stony mountain. Mr Hoggart started the car.

'Why d'you think he's barmy, Tim?'

'Who?'

'Mr Jones.'

'Because of the golf clubs,' Tim said. 'I mean, why would you bring golf clubs to a place like Skua? Everyone knows it's a wild, lonely sort of place with only one town and no proper roads . . .'

'Not everyone, Tim. *He* didn't apparently.'

'That's what's funny. I mean . . .' Tim frowned, trying to put his thoughts in order. 'The golf clubs are new,' he said at last. 'So he must have bought them specially to come on holiday. And you'd think, if you'd gone to the trouble of buying new golf clubs just to go on holiday with, you'd go to the trouble of finding out if there was a golf course, where you were going to . . .'

'I expect there's some perfectly simple explanation, such as he's spending the first half of his holiday here, on Skua, and the second half somewhere else, playing golf.' From the tone of his father's voice, Tim knew he was trying not to sound bored.

'Then why did he ask Mr Tarbutt where the golf course was? He did, I heard him. If he's not mad, then *I* think that's pretty sinister,' Tim said comfortably. 'Don't you think it's sinister, Dad?'

His father smiled at him vaguely, but did not reply.

'Aren't you interested?'

Mr Hoggart said, very apologetically, 'Well – since you ask, no, not really. Sorry, Tim, but I'm more interested in looking for orchids, just at this moment.'

It was Tim's turn to say nothing.

'Does that bore you?' his father asked in a suddenly anxious voice.

'Oh, of course not, Dad,' Tim said at once, doing his best to sound enthusiastic.

Mr Hoggart was an easy man to deceive. 'That's good,' he said, and stopped the car. 'I think we might try over there, on the cliffs. It looks like the right sort of terrain.'

They left the car and took to the peat bog. Round their squelching feet, tiny white flags of bog cotton waved, like the banners of a miniature army. They plodded on towards drier ground, watched by sheep with long, white aristocratic faces and a few highland cattle with terrifying, curved horns. There was no sound except the crying of gulls and the music of water, falling in silver streaks down the brown mountains and rushing in clear, rocky streams across the flatter land to the cliff edge and the sea.

The bog ended and they came to a hollow where the ground was firmer. On the far side of the hollow, sheltered from the cliff edge, was a broken-down crofter's cottage, just four blackened roofless walls and a hole where the door had been. Tim went to explore and found the remains of an iron bedstead, lying on its side among the grass and the sheep dung.

It was the fourth abandoned cottage they had seen since they left the hotel that morning.

'Where did all the people go?' he asked his father, who had got tools out of the rucksack and was digging up spagnum moss to line his specimen boxes.

'De-population.' Mr Hoggart glanced at Tim, sighed, and stopped work to explain. 'The land's poor, so were the people. Their children wanted a better living, so they went away and when their parents grew old and died, there was no one to

farm the croft. Sometimes whole families went, to the mainland, or to America...'

'But it's so nice here,' Tim objected.

'You mightn't think so, if you were starving.'

Tim had thought Skua the most beautiful place he had ever
seen. Now, though it was still beautiful, it seemed somehow
desolate, too.

His father smiled at him. 'We came here to look for orchids,'
he said. 'Remember?'

They were looking for a black orchid – at least, that was how
Mr Hoggart described it to Tim, not bothering his son with
its long, botanical name. He just told him that this black orchid
was very rare, that it had only, so far, been found in parts of
Scandinavia, and that it might not be black at all, but a kind of
wine red or dark purplish colour.

They searched all morning. They found mauve and white
wild orchids, incredibly small and delicate, but no darker
ones. Mr Hoggart could have gone on searching all day, but
by lunch time he judged Tim had had enough. They cleaned
their tools, packed the specimen boxes, and settled down on
the edge of the cliff to watch the sea and eat sandwiches.

Below them, the sea boomed. It was a hollow sound, like
gunfire. 'There must be caves down there,' Tim said. He got
out the map and, tracing the wavy line of the small road they
had taken, stabbed his finger triumphantly on the jutting
headland. 'There *are* caves,' he shouted. 'Look, Dad, it's called
the Point of Caves.'

'A long way down.' Mr Hoggart lay on his stomach and
looked over the edge. 'Sheer,' he said. 'No way down. Not
even for goats.'

Tim was examining the map. 'There's a sort of gully *here* ...'
He looked out to sea, orientating himself by the other islands
which looked, from this distance, curiously unreal, like floating
cardboard castles. 'At the bottom of the gully, there's a cave
called Carlin's Cave. I should think it's about a mile from here.'

'Caves are only exciting in books,' his father said. 'In real life, they're usually a disappointment. Smelly, damp, full of dead sheep . . .'

But Tim was already on his feet, humping his rucksack. They walked along the cliff top, wind in their faces, gulls screaming overhead. Tim's reckoning had been wrong. They came across the gully after about five hundred yards, and suddenly: the ground seemed to open beneath their feet.

A steep, grassy slope went down between rocky sides, and disappeared. There was the sound of water.

'Dangerous,' Mr Hoggart said.

'If you're frightened, you can stay here,' Tim said kindly. He went down the grass on his bottom. Mr Hoggart followed him gingerly. The gully twisted, then opened out on to a flat ledge of grass beside a waterfall which shot out from glistening, black rock. The water fell into a clear, shallow pool, snaked and curled downwards over more rocks, and fell again, out of their sight, with a sound like thunder.

'It's very pleasant here,' Mr Hoggart said hopefully, but Tim had already vanished, further down.

'We can get down the sides of the fall,' he shouted, his voice echoing against the rocky sides of the gully.

Mr Hoggart gave a loud groan and went after his son, working his way down the precipitous sides of the lower waterfall. It was a treacherous climb. The rocky cliff crumbled like plaster in places, and the grassy patches, that looked safe and easy enough, were slippery as an ice rink when he stepped on to them. Mr Hoggart, who was not a climbing man, was sweating when he arrived on a small, shingle beach. He sat on a rock to recover.

Tim was on his hands and knees, scrambling over rocks. 'There's some super stones for my collection. Look, Dad . . .'

He staggered over to his father, carrying a piece of granite flecked with pink and green, the shape of a giant ostrich egg.

'You're not hoping to get that back up the cliff, are you?' Mr Hoggart said.

Tim looked up at the menacing black cliff, which seemed to move against the sky. He grinned. 'Perhaps we'll find something smaller in the cave.'

The beach was triangular: Carlin's Cave was at the apex of the triangle. It was smelly, as Mr Hoggart had said, but it was not a disappointment. The entrance was arched, like the doorway to a cathedral, and inside the walls rose high and seemed to be made up of black columns. The cave went back, deep into the cliff. Tim went in until it was too dark to see. His father shouted and his voice boomed weirdly, with a strange, hollow sound like an organ. When Tim came back, he was looking at his watch.

'Not yet,' Tim pleaded. 'We don't have to go yet. Let me just find some stones.' He searched on the beach and in the cave mouth that was full of great boulders and rock pools between them. The boulders were slippery and Tim splashed into one pool after another, talking fast as he always did when excited. 'This is the most marvellous place – do you suppose it used to be a smuggler's cave? No – it can't be – you couldn't carry smuggler's loot up those cliffs – perhaps no one's ever been here. . . . Oh, *Dad*, do you suppose we're the first people ever to come here?' He stopped, awed. 'The first people since the beginning of the world?'

' Well . . .' His father hesitated. Driven into a rock outside the cave, was a rusty, iron ring, as if someone, sometime, had beached a boat here. A stickler for truth, Mr Hoggart was about to point this out, when a shout from Tim distracted him.

'Look . . . look what I've found, Dad.'

In his excitement, Tim dropped the small stones he had already collected, to pounce on the new one that had caught his eye. It was inside the cave and had been trapped between two small rocks at the side of a pool, wedged so tight by sea or tide that Tim had to hammer at it with a larger stone to get it loose. His father waited impatiently. 'Tim – we really must go,' he said at last.

'Wait ... oh wait ...' Tim gasped as the stone came suddenly loose and would have fallen down the crack between the rocks if he had not jammed his fingers quickly beneath it, grazing his knuckles so badly that he hissed in his breath with pain.

The pain was forgotten in a moment, but when he rushed to his father with his prize, Mr Hoggart was too concerned with his son's bleeding knuckles to be interested in the stone. In any case, he was used to Tim's collection, and, though he tried to enthuse when a new treasure was brought to him, he felt as lukewarm about stones as Tim did about flowers. 'Very pretty,' he said now, 'but – oh goodness – you've made a nasty mess of yourself getting it.'

'You haven't looked at it,' Tim complained. ''Tisn't an ordinary stone.' He scratched at one salt-encrusted edge with his nail. The surface was smooth and ruby red. 'It *is* a ruby,' Tim breathed. 'Dad, I'm sure it's a ruby.'

Mr Hoggart glanced at the dirty stone, about the size of a sixpence, and laughed gently. 'Oh, Tim, Tim ... a ruby that size would be quite valuable.'

Tim scowled at the tone of his father's voice. 'That doesn't mean it isn't one.'

'No – but you don't find rubies on beaches. Oh – it's pretty, or will be when it's cleaned up, but it's a piece of glass or quartz, something like that. I'm no geologist. Tell you what, Tim, we'll see if there's a reference book at the hotel. It'll be fun to look it up, won't it? We'll do that soon as we get back, shall we?'

He spoke coaxingly, smiling at Tim to cheer him up, as if, Tim thought, suddenly savage with disappointment, he was a baby, not a boy twelve years old.

He trailed up the cliffs and back to the car, lagging behind his father all the way, silent and sullen. Mr Hoggart, who was not naturally a noticing man – though tactful and kind whenever he did notice – thought he was just tired.

They met the stranger when they were halfway back to the hotel. Rounding a bend in the pot-holed road, they almost ran into a white Jaguar car, that was slewed sideways, its back wheels in the ditch. A man in dark glasses sat in the driving seat, smoking a cigarette.

Mr Hoggart stopped the Ford and got out. 'Can we help?' he asked. The man stared, not replying until Mr Hoggart repeated his question when he shrugged his shoulders and said, 'She won't budge. Got bogged down trying to turn.' He looked coldly angry, as if this was Mr Hoggart's fault. Tim and his father inspected the back of the car. It was sunk in the boggy ditch, up to its bumper.

'Perhaps we can give you a tow,' Mr Hoggart suggested.

'With Tarbutt's old Ford?' The man laughed and tossed away his cigarette end.

'Oh, surely . . .' Mr Hoggart adjusted his spectacles and looked enthusiastic: he liked to think of himself as a practical man in an emergency. 'If I put it in bottom gear . . .'

'We haven't a tow rope,' Tim said patiently. He looked at the man. 'Have you?'

'No.' The man's expression was suddenly more friendly. 'Stupid not to carry one, on these roads. Though what I really need is a chain and a Land-Rover. If you and your father would kindly give me a lift.'

'Certainly,' Mr Hoggart said. 'Skuaphort?'

'On the way. Perhaps you'd drop me off.' The man got out of his car. 'My name's Smith. You'll be the botanist, staying at the hotel?' He smiled at Mr Hoggart's surprised look. 'Everyone knows everyone else's business on Skua.' He got into the Ford beside Mr Hoggart and said casually to Tim. 'How about you? Going to follow in your father's footsteps?'

'No.' Tim, who was still feeling resentful, scowled at the

back of his father's head. 'I'm not going to be a *botanist*,' he said scornfully. 'I'm going to be something useful, like a *policeman*.'

Mr Smith raised his eyebrows. 'Do you really think that is a more useful profession?' he asked, very dryly.

Mr Hoggart coughed. An extremely polite man himself, he was always embarrassed by rudeness. He tried to apologize for Tim. 'He's been a bit bored today, I'm afraid. Flowers aren't really much in his line . . .' He smiled over his shoulder at his son in a kindly way that made Tim feel ashamed. 'He prefers stones. In fact, he's got quite an interesting collection. Tim – why don't you show Mr Smith the one you got today? The – er – ruby.'

'Ruby?' Mr Smith turned round in his seat. Tim could not see his eyes, because of the dark glasses, but he felt that their gaze was suddenly intent.

'Dad says it isn't one,' he said slowly, rather reluctant to expose his treasure to someone else's judgement.

'Show me,' Mr Smith said. 'As a matter of fact, I know a bit about precious stones.'

He held out his hand and Tim gave him the little stone. Smith turned it over thoughtfully, his dark glasses pushed up on his nose. 'Well . . .' he said, and seemed to hesitate. Tim felt excitement mounting inside him.

'Gate, Tim,' his father said, stopping the car. Tim tumbled out, opened the gate, closed it, and almost fell back into the Ford. Then his heart sank. Mr Smith was shaking his head.

'Afraid not, old chap. Could be a bit of jasper quartz I suppose, though that isn't common round here. Or some sort of crystal, like red copper ore. But I'm very much afraid,' – he smiled at Tim regretfully – 'that when it's cleaned up, it'll turn out to be just a piece of red glass.'

'Oh,' Tim said. 'Thank you.' He took the stone and thrust it deep into his pocket.

'Sorry, old chap,' Mr Smith said.

Tim stared out of the window. Disappointment blurred his vision. He began to hum under his breath to show Mr Smith and his father that he didn't really care.

The road led round the side of Ben Luin and came down to the sea and a small beach where a tent was pitched. The tent had been extended at one end to make a more permanent, if slightly makeshift dwelling, by a heavy, dark tarpaulin fastened over some kind of frame. A piece of piping protruded from the top, to make a rough chimney. A Land-Rover stood on a patch of grass between the tent and the Ford.

'If you'll drop me here,' Mr Smith said. As Mr Hoggart slowed the car, a boy of about Tim's age came out of the tent and stared. The Ford stopped and Mr Smith got out and waved to the boy. 'Alistair,' he shouted, 'your father at home?' Without waiting for an answer, he turned to Mr Hoggart. 'Will Campbell's a friend of mine. Lobster fisherman. Camps here during the summer season. Bit of an eccentric, but a good chap. He'll give me a hand with the old Jag.'

Mr Hoggart nodded and smiled as if he were not quite sure what reply to make.

'I'm grateful for the lift,' Mr Smith said.

'Glad we came along.' Mr Hoggart smiled again, and moved his hand to the gear lever, but Mr Smith seemed reluctant to take his hand off the side of the car. 'Oh, well ...' he said vaguely. He sighed and stared at the tent. The boy had disappeared now. 'Must be getting along, I suppose,' Mr Smith said, but showed no signs of doing so. Instead he poked his head inside the car and said to Tim, 'Tell you what, old chap, one good turn deserves another. As I said, I know a bit about stones – sort of amateur geologist, as a matter of fact. If you like, I'll take that stone of yours home with me. I've got all the right gear, microscopes, that sort of thing. I'll get it cleaned up a bit and have a good look at it for you.'

'Really, that is *most* kind,' Mr Hoggart said. 'Isn't it, Tim? Tim ...'

Tim put his hand in his pocket. His fingers touched the stone, curled round it – and then stayed still. For no reason – for absolutely no reason that he could think of at that moment – he suddenly felt an enormous reluctance to part with his useless treasure. And it wasn't just the sort of reluctance he would ordinarily have felt about parting with a newly acquired possession, not just the simple desire to keep the stone to himself a little longer, to touch and admire it. . . . Tim was sure he would have conquered such a babyish feeling. No – it was something else altogether, something to do with the way Mr Smith was smiling and stretching out his hand, not only confident that his very kind offer would be accepted, but also – suddenly Tim was sure of it – very eager that it should be. Why? He didn't seem the sort of man who would, in the ordinary way, be so terribly keen to put himself to any sort of trouble for a boy . . .

'No thank you,' Tim said loudly.

His father turned to look at him in surprise and some embarrassment. Tim looked squarely back at him.

'I want to show it to Janey, first,' he said.

4

MR HOGGART HAS AN ACCIDENT

'I CAN'T see whether it's pretty or not,' Janey said. 'It's too dirty.'

She saw with her fingers which felt and stroked and patted, learning the shape of the stone so well that she would always, Tim knew, be able to pick it out from all the other stones he had found since he had come to Skua. 'Perhaps you could clean it up with gin,' she suggested. 'Mum cleans her engagement ring with gin, and that's got rubies in it.' She put the stone back into the white cardboard box that held the rest of Tim's collection. 'Tell me about Carlin's Cave again.'

Tim told her. She listened eagerly, her head on one side. 'I wish I could go there.'

'You couldn't possibly. It's terribly dangerous going down the cliff. Even for people who can see.'

Janey said nothing. Once, if someone had told her there was something she could not do – would never be able to do – she would have thrown herself on the floor, screaming and kicking, in a terrible tantrum. But that was when she was younger: now she was nine years old. Tim knew she minded about not being able to climb down the cliff because she had gone suddenly quiet, but a stranger would not have known.

He said, 'I don't suppose Dad would've let you go anyway, because you're a girl.'

'Girls can climb as well as boys,' Janey said. 'And they can find things, too. I found lots of shells on the beach and a lovely sheep's skull. I'm going to collect sheeps' skulls.'

'Whatever for?'

'To put things in, of course,' Janey said in a surprised voice. 'They're awfully useful for that.'

'I suppose so,' Tim said doubtfully, looking with some distaste at the white skull grinning on the pillow of Janey's bed. 'I can't see there's much point in collecting them, though. I mean there are just hundreds and hundreds of sheeps' skulls on Skua, lying about all over the place. You ought to collect unusual things – like stones, or Dad's orchids.'

'Orchids aren't useful, though. Sheeps' skulls are,' Janey said. She paused. 'I did find something unusual today. Mum says it's a fossil. I'm going to collect fossils and keep them in my sheep's skull.'

She produced a flat piece of rock from her pocket. Tim turned it over. 'Looks like a piece of slate to me.'

Janey sniffed. 'You've not looked properly. You never look properly. It's got a leaf in it, a fossilized leaf, can't you see?'

She took his finger and traced it up the spine and along the radiating veins. It was only then that he saw it: the shape embossed on the stone, a fragile skeleton of a leaf that had got pressed into the rock, millions and millions of years ago.

'I don't know how people who can only see, can tell what things are,' Janey said.

They went down to supper with their parents. Their table was by the window looking out on to the harbour. The only other person in the dining-room was Mr Jones, sitting at his solitary table and chewing a toffee while he waited for his soup to be brought to him.

Janey said, 'Someone came and played with me, on the beach.'

Mrs Hoggart looked surprised. 'Janey – there was no one there except us.'

Janey put her head on one side as she felt round her plate for the spoon. 'Not while you were awake. But you went to sleep. It was while you were asleep that *she* came.'

'Who?' Tim asked.

'I don't know her name. She knew mine, though. I was looking for shells and she said, "Hallo, Janey," and gave me the stone with the leaf in it. She showed me how to feel it.'

Tim was interested. 'What did you talk about? Didn't she tell you her name?'

Janey shook her head. 'I did ask, but she just laughed. A sort of whispery laugh. Then she let me feel her face and her clothes – she had a funny long skirt on. I asked her several times what her name was, but she just said Ssh. I think she was scared Mum would wake up. So we looked for shells for a bit, and when Mum woke up, she went away.'

'Why didn't you tell me, Janey?' Mrs Hoggart said.

'Because she wanted to be secret. If she'd heard me telling you, she might've made up her mind not to come again.'

'But you said she'd gone away!' Mrs Hoggart looked at her husband with an expression Tim recognized.

Janey couldn't see the expression, but she could hear the tone of her mother's voice. She said, indignantly. 'Only hiding where you couldn't see her. I knew she was still there, because she made a bird sound to tell me.'

'*I* didn't hear anything, darling,' Mrs Hoggart said, in the special, bright, humouring voice she sometimes used to Janey.

Janey scowled. 'Don't talk to me in that silly way. She didn't *want* you to hear. Only me. And I *did* hear. I can hear things other people can't, you know I can, you stupid.'

'Don't be rude to your mother.' Mr Hoggart, who was anxious Janey should not be spoiled, just because she was blind, spoke to her firmly. 'And eat up your soup, we're all waiting for you,' he said.

Janey went very red. Beneath the tablecloth, Tim felt for her free hand and squeezed it sympathetically: he knew Janey was often lonely, and that the people she invented to play with, were very real and important to her. But Janey must have guessed that he didn't believe in this girl on the beach any more than her parents did, because she wrenched her hand away angrily, and burst into tears.

As soon as supper was over, Mrs Hoggart took Janey to bed.

'Exhausted, poor darling,' she said, when she came down and joined Tim and his father who were playing chess by the fire in the hotel lounge. 'The wind's getting up, so I bolted her window. I think, really, we ought to ask if she could eat earlier, having supper with us means she stays up long past her bed time. Now, where *did* I put my knitting? I'm sure I had it earlier on – yes, I did, I remember sitting here knitting when Janey and I came back from the beach. What can have happened to it?'

Neither Tim nor his father spoke, and she did not expect them to, being the sort of person who always conducted this sort of conversation with herself.

'Oh, here it is, under the cushion. I'm sure that's not where I put it. Who did put it there, I wonder?'

This time Tim did answer her. 'Mr Jones, I expect,' he said. 'He was sitting there before supper. Left a lot of toffee papers on the ground and Janey picked them up and packed them into her sheep's skull.' He laughed. 'Janey says she's going to call him Toffee Papers. That's a good name for him, isn't it?'

His mother frowned and whispered. 'Ssh, dear. He's only just the other side of the passage, in the little bar . . .'

Mr Hoggart stood up. 'I'd better go and say good night to Janey. I won't be long, Tim.'

'Shouldn't bother, dear, she's probably asleep already,' Mrs Hoggart said, but her husband had gone before she had finished her sentence.

'He's sorry he was cross with her at supper,' Tim said.

'Yes, I know. But it's difficult . . .' Mrs Hoggart stopped and sighed. She gazed into the fire for a minute and then her expression changed: she was thinking of something else. 'Tim,' she said softly, 'I'm sure I've seen him before . . .'

'Who?' Tim was only half listening. His father wanted him to be good at chess, and though Tim did not much care whether he was good or not, he wanted to please his father and so he stared hard at the board, trying to work out his next move.

'Toffee Papers. Messy habit, that . . .' Mrs Hoggart was gazing thoughtfully in front of her. 'Funny thing *is*, I know his face. Not well, mind you . . .'

'As if he was someone you'd seen several times on a bus?' Tim suggested. His mother had a good memory for faces, but could seldom put names to them.

'Well, no. I don't think it was a bus . . .'

'Train, then. The train up to London.' Tim abandoned the chess board and launched into this game, which he much preferred: he and his mother shared a taste for what Mr Hoggart called useless speculation. 'The telly?' Tim said 'or the newspaper?'

His mother's eyes widened. 'I'm not sure . . . perhaps . . .' Suddenly she struck the heels of her hand against her forehead and cried excitedly, 'That's it, I think I've got it, Tim. It was . . .'

But what – or where – it was, Tim didn't discover. There was a loud wail from upstairs and his mother gasped Janey's name, and shot out of her chair like a jack-in-the-box.

'It's O.K. Dad's there,' Tim shouted, but she had gone from the room. He picked up her knitting which had fallen to the floor, and followed her. If Janey had had a nightmare, she would want him. She loved her mother and father, but when she woke from a bad dream, it was Tim she turned to . . .

But this was not a bad dream. It was real. When Tim reached the bedroom, Mrs Hoggart was kneeling beside her husband who was lying on the floor. He was lying very still. Janey was sitting up in bed. She wasn't crying, but she was shaking all over. Tim went to her and took her hands. 'There was someone in the room,' she whispered, and pressed close to him.

Mrs Hoggart looked up. She was pale, but her voice was controlled and gentle. 'Only Daddy, darling. He was coming to say good night and he had an accident. He must have slipped.'

'Is he dead?' Janey asked.

'No, my darling, of course not. I think he's banged his poor head. We'll have to put him to bed and get a doctor. Tim, dear, would you run down and ask Mr Tarbutt?'

She was speaking slowly, to quieten Janey, but her eyes were frightened.

Mr Tarbutt was already coming up the stairs. 'Doctor!' he said in a bewildered voice, when Tim explained what had happened. 'Well, I'm afraid . . .' He ran up the last few stairs and into the room. 'I'm afraid it's Wednesday,' he said.

'Wednesday?' Mrs Hoggart repeated, staring at Mr Tarbutt as if she feared he was mad. 'What's Wednesday got to do with it?'

'Doctor comes Tuesdays and Fridays,' Mr Tarbutt explained. 'Otherwise, in an emergency, we have to telephone the mainland.' He knelt beside Mr Hoggart. 'I was in the Medical Corps during the war. Long time ago, I know, but I keep my hand in round here . . . cuts . . . sprained ankles . . . I even set a broken arm last summer. . . .' While he was speaking, his fingers explored Mr Hoggart's head. 'Got a whacking great lump there. I should guess he slid on the rug, fell backwards, and knocked himself out on the bed. Nasty things, these iron bedsteads, I wish we could afford to replace them.' He sat back on his heels and looked at Mr Hoggart thoughtfully. He looked peaceful, but he was breathing loudly, in a snoring sort of way. 'Concussed himself, maybe,' Mr Tarbutt said.

He frowned across the room at Tim, who was sitting beside Janey, stroking her hair to comfort her. 'Better get the lass out of here,' Mr Tarbutt said. He got to his feet, crossed the room in a stride, and picked Janey up. She hated to be lifted by strangers, but before she could protest he had whisked her next door, into her parents' room, and deposited her on their bed. 'Stay with her, now,' he said to Tim.

Janey nestled in Tim's arms, her face buried in his shoulder.

He sat still, holding her and straining his ears to hear what was going on outside the door, which Mr Tarbutt had closed behind him. There was a confused babble of voices and steps running up and down the stairs. He could hear Mr Tarbutt, and then his wife answering him, but not what they said. He wished he could be out there, doing something to help, but he couldn't leave Janey. She was so still that once he thought she had fallen asleep, but the moment he relaxed his grip on her she clutched at him fiercely until he held her tight and safe again.

His arms had begun to ache and it seemed as if hours must have passed – though, looking at his watch, he saw it was only twenty minutes – when the door opened and his mother came in.

She had her coat on. 'Darlings,' she said, 'are you all right?' Without waiting for an answer, she sat on the edge of the bed and told them that Mr Tarbutt had telephoned the doctor at Oban, who had said Mr Hoggart should be taken to hospital at once. 'It's probably nothing much,' she said. 'But they always take X-rays when you have had a bad bang on the head, and they can only do that in hospital. So the Emergency Service is sending a helicopter.'

'A helicopter?' Tim said. 'A helicopter . . .?' For a moment he forgot his father in a rush of lovely, hot excitement. 'Where will it land, Mum?'

'At the back of the hotel. There's a flat field. You'll be able to see it land and take off. That'll be fun, won't it, Janey darling?'

Janey loved the sound of aeroplanes: sometimes, on Sunday mornings, Mr Hoggart drove to London Airport, just so she could stand on the waving base and listen.

Janey said, 'Aren't we all going in the helicopter? I *want* to go in the helicopter.'

Mrs Hoggart took her hand. 'I'm sorry, darling, there just isn't room. I'm going with Dad, but you and Tim will have to stay here. You'll be all right. Mrs Tarbutt says she'll look after you. She's very nice, you like her, don't you?'

'I do not,' Janey said. 'She called me a poor little thing. I heard her.'

Mrs Hoggart looked helplessly at Tim who shrugged his shoulders. There was nothing much you could do about stupid grown-ups who were sorry for Janey – except, he thought, suddenly grinning, make them look after her for a bit!

'She won't be calling you that by the time Mum comes back,' he said. 'She'll be calling you a ghastly little horror. When's the helicopter coming, Mum?'

'Any minute.' Mrs Hoggart went to the window. 'You should get a grand view from here.'

Janey slid off the bed. 'It's coming,' she cried. 'I can hear it.'

Mrs Hoggart kissed them good-bye and left them at the open window, one listening, one watching, while the helicopter came whirring in, bumping its wheels gingerly on the rough field and their unconscious father was carried out of the hotel and loaded into the flying ambulance like . . . like a long parcel, Tim told Janey, who laughed and began to wave excitedly, as if her father was going off on holiday, instead of to hospital. 'Is he waving back?' she asked Tim. He didn't answer, and she said, suddenly frowning, 'Why didn't he say good-bye to me?'

'He . . . well . . . he wasn't feeling very well,' Tim said awkwardly, and then all the excitement left him and he stood, silent and apprehensive while the helicopter took off, looking, as it grew smaller and smaller, like some strange, prehistoric insect, whirring up into the yellow and scarlet sunset.

5

THERE WAS SOMEONE ELSE IN
THE ROOM

MRS TARBUTT was a kindly, sentimental woman. There were tears of pity in her eyes as she entered the room and saw the two children standing forlornly by the window. 'Oh, you poor lambs,' she cried, and would have taken Janey in her arms if Tim had not got in her way. He knew how Janey reacted to what she called 'sloppy hugging and kissing'.

Mrs Tarbutt brushed the back of her hand across her eyes and said, trying hard to sound cheerful, 'Well, beddy-byes in a minute, I suppose. But perhaps you'd like to come downstairs first and have a hot drink by the fire in the lounge. Something nice and milky to settle you.'

'I don't like milk,' Janey said.

'Oh. Well . . .'

'I'd like a Coke,' Janey said. 'And some cheese and pickled onions. But I don't want it in the lounge. I want to have it in the bar.'

She smiled to herself, and Tim knew why. Janey knew children were not allowed in the bar. She also knew that at this moment Mrs Tarbutt would not deny her anything.

'Well . . . perhaps just this once,' Mrs Tarbutt said. She smiled rather weakly at Tim, and took Janey's hand. 'We'll go down to the bar then, my lamb.'

Politely but firmly, Janey removed her hand. 'I can go myself.'

'She'll be all right,' Tim said quickly. 'Once she's been shown round, she can always find her way after.'

Mrs Tarbutt was sensible enough to believe him. As she preceded them down the stairs, she glanced back nervously at

48

Janey, but made no attempt to help her. Downstairs, Janey let Tim guide her into the bar, because this room was strange to her, and help her on to a high stool at the counter. She sat, perched, her long hair flowing over her nightdress. 'Two Cokes, I think,' Mrs Tarbutt said.

'And cheese and pickled onions,' Janey added.

Behind the counter, Mr Tarbutt raised his eyebrows, but he turned to the plastic dome under which the cheese was kept.

'Cheese lies heavy on the stomach at night,' Toffee Papers said. 'And pickles are poison.' He was sitting at a table with another man: apart from the Tarbutts and the children, there was no one else in the room.

'I like cheese and pickled onions,' Janey said, turning round on her stool and frowning in the direction of the voice.

'Dad says she can digest iron nails,' Tim said.

Toffee Papers said no more. But his eyes bulged as he saw Janey with a bowl of onions before her. She ate twelve very large ones, one after the other.

Tim drank his Coke. He said to Mr Tarbutt, 'Will they ring up from the hospital, about Dad?'

'In the morning, I daresay.' Mr Tarbutt smiled at Tim. 'Don't you worry. He's in good hands, he'll be all right.'

'I still can't figure out how it happened,' Mrs Tarbutt said.

Her husband winked at Tim. 'Too much polish on the floors, Mother.'

Mrs Tarbutt bridled. 'I keep a clean house, I hope. But not dangerous – no polish under the rugs. I don't know how he came to slip.'

'Someone knows,' Janey said. She dipped a searching finger into the empty onion bowl and withdrew it with a sigh. 'There was someone in the room.'

Tim said, 'That was Dad. I expect you . . .'

'Not Dad,' Janey said, very loudly and clearly. 'Someone else, first.'

There was silence in the bar. Tim looked round. Toffee

Papers and the man with him were watching Janey intently.

'Oh, the poor lassie,' Mrs Tarbutt cried. 'She must have had a terrible fright, waking up like that.' She spoke to Janey very gently. 'There wasn't anyone else, dear. Who could there have been? Mr Tarbutt and I were in the kitchen, washing the dishes . . .'

Toffee Papers cleared his throat. 'And *we* were in the bar all the time. Me and Mr Campbell. No one else here. No one came in, either, or we'd have seen them pass the door. Isn't that right, Campbell?'

Campbell nodded. He was a thin man with a thin, bearded face.

'There *was* someone else in the room,' Janey said. 'I *heard*.'

Her face had gone red and stubborn and Tim was embarrassed. Janey's hearing was sharp and quick. She was not often mistaken, but in this case, she must be. Except the people in this room now, there was no one else in the hotel. And they had all been together, the Tarbutts in the kitchen and Toffee Papers and this other man in the bar. Even if they hadn't been, what reason could any of them have had for going up to Janey's bedroom? No – she had had a nightmare, that was all. She often had nightmares about people in her room, and, waking up as she must have done when her father slipped and fell, the nightmare had got confused with reality.

He said, 'It was a bad dream, Janey. Just a bad dream.'

Mrs Tarbutt looked relieved. 'Of course it was, poor love. Who'd want to come creeping into your room and frightening you?'

'A burglar might,' Janey said.

Toffee Papers laughed merrily. 'Your sister's got a lively imagination, young man,' he said, to Tim. 'Mind you, I'm not surprised.' Broadly smiling, he addressed the rest of the company. 'Got a couple of girls myself – I know all about it, I can tell you. The things they make up! You'd be surprised!' He laughed again and slapped his short, fat thigh. 'I'll tell you one thing, girlie. I'll bet my bottom dollar there's no burglars on Skua. Nothing to steal, that's why!'

'It certainly would not be a very lucrative profession on this island,' Mr Tarbutt said.

His wife gave a half sigh. 'Indeed no . . .' She smiled rather sadly at Janey. 'People are poor and honest round here. So you can stop worrying, my lamb.'

Janey said nothing. She scowled and scowled. Embarrassed, Tim slipped off his stool. 'I think she should go to bed now, Mrs Tarbutt.'

'That's right,' Mr Jones said, picking at his bottom teeth with his thumb nail. 'Bed's the best place.'

Janey went up, stumping angrily on every stair. When Tim got into bed beside her, she turned her back on him, pulling the bedclothes over her head. 'Pig. Unbeliever,' she said in a muffled voice.

Tim sighed and switched off the bedside light.

A little later, he heard her chuckle.

'*He*'ll believe it,' she said.

'Who'll believe what?' Tim asked, yawning.

'*Dad*'ll believe in the burglar. Because he must've seen him, mustn't he?'

Tim stared into the darkness. Outside, the wind was up and rattling the window his mother had bolted earlier. Indoors, the hotel seemed full of small, creaky sounds. He said, '*If* there was a burglar. If, if, *if* . . .' There was no response from beside him and he went on, suddenly exasperated, 'You're always making things up. Like that girl on the beach . . .'

Up at Luinpool, the witch's daughter stirred in her sleep as the Land-Rover stopped outside the yard gate, dropped its passenger and drove off again. She opened her eyes for a brief second when the handful of stones rattled against Mr Smith's window, but closed them again almost at once and smiled to herself, half asleep, half awake, dreaming of Janey. The wind, approaching gale force now, whipped the waves on the loch and howled down the chimney of Perdita's bedroom, drowning the sound of the men's voices in the room beneath.

'No one saw you?'
'Only the blind child, but she . . .'
'He'll know, though. When he comes round . . .'
'*If* he comes round.'
'If he doesn't,' – Mr Smith's voice was grim – 'then you're for it, anyway. Campbell won't stand for murder. You'll have to clear out.'
'How? There's no steamer for days.'
'Campbell will take you off. Tomorrow, with luck. He won't question *that*. And as long as Hoggart recovers, he'll keep his mouth shut.'
'What did you tell Campbell?'
'Just that the boy had picked up something of yours that you might like to get back. Privately, without fuss.'
'Oh – for God's sake. Couldn't the kid have kept the stone?'
'It was a risk.'
'This has turned out a bigger one.'
'It needn't have been. If you hadn't bungled it . . .'
'I didn't mean to hurt him, Smithie . . .' Mr Jones's voice was suddenly despairing. 'But he came blundering in . . . I only pushed him out of my way . . .'
'If it was an accident, you should have stood your ground.'
'The kid screamed and I – I lost my nerve. Ducked out and hid in the bathroom till the coast was clear and I could get back to the bar. Easy enough, no one suspected anything.'
'They will tomorrow. When he comes round and they get on to the police . . .'
Mr Jones made a low, groaning sound.
'There's only one thing now,' Mr Smith said. 'Lie low – disappear.' He laughed suddenly. 'People do disappear. They fall off cliff edges, drown. . . . With luck, maybe they'll think

you're dead.' He paused a minute, then added softly, 'As long as there's nothing to connect this little trouble with . . . with our other business.'

'Connect *me* with *you*, that's what you mean, isn't it Smithie?'

'If you like,' Mr Smith said evenly.

There was a silence. Then Mr Jones said, 'I suppose you'd like me to clear off now? Walk into a bog – over a cliff – that would suit you nicely, wouldn't it?'

'Maybe it would.' Mr Smith sounded apologetic. 'But I won't drive you out – not tonight. You can kip down here. There are rooms kept locked upstairs.'

'What about the kid and the old woman?'

'As long as you're quiet, it'll be safe enough. Annie only goes upstairs to sleep, and the child doesn't pry,' Mr Smith said.

Perdita cried out as they reached the top of the stairs. Mr Smith motioned the other man to stay still, and opened her door.

She was sitting up, blinking, rosy with sleep.

'I heard someone,' she said.

'Only me.' Mr Smith closed the door with his foot. He stood, candle in hand, looking down at her. 'Been awake long?' he asked casually.

'I don't know. On and off.' She frowned. 'I think I heard a car,' she said doubtfully.

'Will Campbell,' Mr Smith said. 'The wind's high and he came to tell me he'd changed my mooring.'

She nodded: this satisfied her. Mr Smith kept a small ketch in the bay where Will Campbell pitched his tent. 'Will you take me out in your boat one day?' she asked, yawning.

'Maybe. If you go to sleep now.'

'Where will we go?'

'Round the islands.' A board on the landing creaked as Mr

Jones shifted his position. Mr Smith coughed and sat down on the edge of the bed. 'Perhaps we'll go further,' he said.

'Where to?'

'Lie down and shut your eyes and I'll tell you,' Mr Smith said.

Perdita snuggled down. Mr Smith looked at her rather helplessly. He was not accustomed to telling bedtime stories. 'Well...' he began, 'well...'

'Go on,' Perdita said.

He sighed. 'Well ... we'll get provisions and charts and we'll sail south. Yes, south. We'll sail south for a year and a day until we get to a tropical island.'

'Like Skua?'

Mr Smith pulled a face. 'A bit warmer, I hope. It's hot in the tropics, the sun shines all the time and it hardly ever rains. Only at night, sometimes, to wash everything clean. There are coral reefs and palm trees and – er – parrots.'

'What are parrots?' she murmured.

'Birds. Beautiful birds, all colours of the rainbow, pink, green, purple.... Some of them have crests on their heads like little crowns. All sailors have parrots...' He paused. 'Are you asleep, Perdita?'

'Yes,' she said, very sleepily.

Mr Smith smiled to himself and went on in a soft, monotonous voice until she really was asleep, and then, to please himself, he went on talking a little longer about this tropical island where the sun shone and the cold wind never blew, where they would ride at anchor inside a coral reef and live on coconuts.

Outside on the landing, Mr Jones got cramp in his foot from waiting.

6

THE GIRL ON THE BEACH

THINGS always look different in the morning. That dark shape behind the bedroom door, so frightening at night, is just a hanging coat when daylight comes. When Tim woke, the bright, morning sunlight was falling through the window and Janey's burglar seemed no more than a wild, improbable dream...

And to make it even more improbable, even more dreamlike, there was Mrs Tarbutt at the door, plump and ordinary and beaming with good news. Mrs Hoggart had telephoned early, while the children were still asleep, to say their father was much better. He had recovered consciousness and was now sleeping normally, under sedation. 'That was a nasty old bang he gave his head apparently,' Mrs Tarbutt said, stooping to pick up Tim's clothes, scattered untidily on the floor. 'But nothing serious, praise the Lord. Just a bit of concussion. He'll be right as rain in a day or two, though he's got to be kept quiet, of course. Your Mummy's going to find a nice hotel in Oban and she'll be over to fetch you on the steamer, in five days' time. Now...' Mrs Tarbutt smiled. 'What about breakfast? Porridge and eggs?'

'Two eggs,' Janey said. 'I like two eggs, hard on the outside and runny in the middle.'

'Please,' Tim prompted her.

'Please. Mrs Tarbutt, did Dad say about the...'

Tim kicked her under the bedclothes and she gave a little yelp that made Mrs Tarbutt look at him in a shocked way. He said quickly, 'She wants to know if Dad remembers how he banged his head.'

'Oh, no, dear, he's not well enough to talk yet.' Mrs Tarbutt looked at Janey who was rubbing her leg and scowling. Her expression was pitying, and Tim's heart sank: he knew what her voice would sound like to Janey as she said tenderly, 'Shall I help you get dressed, my lamb?'

Tim felt Janey go stiff beside him. 'I can manage perfectly well, thank you,' she said. Her voice was icy and Tim knew there was no danger, now, that she would ask Mrs Tarbutt any more questions about the burglar – or, indeed, say anything to her at all that was not absolutely necessary. Once someone had insulted Janey by offering to dress her, or cut up her food, or do any of the things that she had struggled so hard to learn to do for herself, she became cold and silent with them. And although, when Mrs Tarbutt looked hurt, Tim was sorry – because after all, she had only meant to be kind – he was relieved, too. If Janey persisted in her ridiculous story about the burglar, Mrs Tarbutt would only laugh. And Tim hated anyone to laugh at Janey.

After breakfast, they went to the bay where Janey had looked for shells the day before. It was some way from the hotel but Janey was a good walker, Tim assured Mrs Tarbutt, who seemed doubtful about letting them go alone and was only persuaded to make sandwiches for their lunch after Tim had coaxed for a good half hour. Even then she felt impelled to extract a number of promises from Tim before she let them go. He was to look after Janey, not to wander too far, not to climb any mountains or cliffs, to keep an eye on his watch and not to come back too late for tea . . .

'I'm surprised she didn't tell me not to *breathe*,' he said glumly, when they finally got away. 'How old does she think I am? Five?'

They crossed the stream by the broken bridge and climbed upwards. Sheep lifted their heads to watch them pass, and, from the top of the ridge, someone else was watching too. When they had breasted the ridge and were walking downhill, across the peat bog to the bay, she came out from behind a rock and ran after them. She ran as a hare runs, stopping and freezing still from time to time, so that her brown skirt and green scarf merged into the colours of the hillside. If Tim had looked back, he would not have known someone was following them.

But follow she did, quiet and bright-eyed and eager. When they reached the bay, she hid among the dunes and watched. Tim found a piece of planking at the water's edge and began to build a sand car for his sister. He threw up a mound of damp sand and she sat inside it, while he patted it into shape around her. After a little, his enthusiasm for this project clearly died and he began to cast longing glances towards the great rock in the middle of the bay. Then, turning his back on temptation, he began to dig more energetically, until the car grew as big as a Rolls-Royce or a Cadillac. Janey got out and he showed her how to make wheels. She became absorbed in this task, and Tim's eyes returned to the rock. He stood, looking at it, his hands in his pockets, and then squatted down beside his sister and seemed to be talking to her urgently. Perdita saw Janey nod her head. Tim stood up and began to run towards the rock.

Perdita waited, her heart thumping. Janey was decorating the bonnet of the car with shells, and singing to herself. When Tim had disappeared round the far side of the rock, Perdita came out from the dunes and crept closer. About ten yards away from Janey, she stopped, pursed her lips, and made a sound like a bird. Janey put her head on one side and laughed. 'I thought you'd come,' she said.

Perdita went to her and stood close, so that Janey could touch her skirt.

'Go on,' Janey said. 'Say something. You *can* talk, can't you?'

Perdita nodded. In her dream last night she had talked to Janey, but now the words seemed trapped in her throat.

'Are you dumb?' Janey said, and gave her skirt a little tug.

Perdita trembled. Then she bent to whisper 'No' in Janey's

ear, and at once jumped back out of the child's reach, shy as a savage.

Sensing her timidity, though not understanding the cause of it, Janey spoke coaxingly. 'What's your name?' She waited, her head on one side. 'Please – won't you tell me your name?'

Perdita gave a little gasp, and told her.

Janey smiled. 'That's pretty. How do you spell it?'

'I . . . I don't know.'

'Don't know?'

'I can't . . .' Perdita began. Then excitement seized her. She crouched beside Janey. 'Can you read and write? Can you teach me?'

Janey said slowly, 'Braille – I can do Braille. But that's not . . .'

'*Letters*,' Perdita said. 'Can you show me letters?' She was shivering with eagerness. She picked up a flat shell and thrust it into Janey's hand. 'Look – write in the sand. Write my name.'

Janey hesitated. 'I'm not very good at ordinary letters. I mean, I know the shape, but writing's hard. You can't feel what you've done.'

'You can feel in the sand,' Perdita said. '*Please*, Janey . . .'

Janey put down the shell. 'I can do it best with my finger, I think.' Slowly and carefully, she drew a rather shaky P in the sand.

Perdita looked at it. 'What's that?'

'P. P for Perdita.'

Perdita laughed. 'Let *me* . . .' She copied the P, over and over. 'Now *your* name.'

Janey grinned suddenly. 'J,' she said. 'J is for Janey. And for Jam. And A is for Apple. That's how you learn . . .' She wrote her name in the sand and Perdita watched her, repeating what Janey said. 'N is for Nuts. E is for Egg. Don't you go to school?' Janey asked.

'No. They won't let me,' Perdita said, and at once Janey wanted to know who 'they' were and why they should stop her going to school, but Perdita was too impatient to get on with her lesson to say more than, 'Oh, Mr Smith thinks I'll carry tales. He likes to be private. Please, Janey – oh please write some more. Write me your brother's name.'

'T,' Janey began. 'T for Tomato, I for Ink, M for Mother . . .'

'Tim,' Perdita said. 'Tim.' She repeated his name loudly and excitedly because she had just understood how the sound of the letters went together to form the word, but Janey who could not really understand that this might be an entirely new discovery for anyone, thought she must be calling him.

'Is Tim coming back already?' she asked. 'He said he was going exploring up on the big rock. Can you see him?'

Perdita looked towards the rock – the same rock she sat upon every week, when she watched for the steamer. A blustery wind had blown clouds up from the west, covering the sun and making the day much colder, but Perdita felt cold for another reason. 'I can't exactly *see* him,' she said, and then began to tremble. 'He's hurt,' she said. 'I can feel that he's hurt . . .'

The great rock was like a castle, a fortress. The basalt rocks formed towers and turrets. Standing at the seaward end of the rock, Tim felt like a feudal chieftain, scanning the green sea for enemy ships. It would be a marvellous place to defend. Inside the outer ring of rock, there was a sheltered expanse of purple heather and soft turf, patterned here and there with flowers. There was even a water supply – necessary if you were going to defend a fortress: small streams making their way towards the precipitous edge and tinkling over in tiny waterfalls. Tim scrambled down a little way and lay on his stomach to look over the battlements of his castle. Along to his left, water was falling from higher up on to a rocky promontory with a patch of grass beside it. It looked inviting, and Tim had a sudden desire to see if he could reach it. The sides of the rock looked sheer, but there was a narrow ledge, two or three inches wide, leading to the waterfall.

He let himself cautiously down, until his toes touched this ledge. Then he flattened himself against the side of the rock and inched sideways like a crab. He was almost at the waterfall when a stone rolled beneath him. He threw himself sideways, twisting his ankle. For a terrifying second, his foot seemed to give way beneath him and he might have fallen, if his frantic fingers had not found a handhold, a crack in the rock. Precariously clinging, he looked down and saw the dislodged stone bounce on the jagged rocks beneath him and disappear in the churning sea . . .

He felt sick. Sea, rock and sky seemed to turn about him and he closed his eyes until the giddiness passed. Then he forced himself to open them and forced himself to move, clinging like a fly to the rock, one terrifying step, then another, until he reached the flat ledge of grass he had been making for.

He collapsed upon it, cold and sweaty from fear and the pain in his foot. The pain was like knives, like fire, shooting up his leg, up his whole body. There was a whirring in his head and he seemed to be swimming away into darkness . . .

Something hard and cold touched his face. He opened his eyes and saw a girl's face above him. She wore something round her neck, dangling on a piece of string: it was this that had swung forward to touch his face as she bent over him. As he stirred, she gave a little cry and would have jerked away if he had not caught hold of the string and held her fast. Her eyes dilated with a wild look: he made a great effort, pulled himself up and threw her down beside him. She lay under the weight of his arm, shivering like a trapped bird.

'I'm sorry,' he said. 'I don't want to hurt you. But you mustn't go away.'

Janey, he thought, *Janey*. How long had he been unconscious? The thought frightened him. Janey was sensible, she had promised to stay exactly where he had left her, but she was only nine and time dragged when you were waiting. Suppose she wandered off, looking for him? He had told her the danger, but had she understood it? How could you really understand the danger of rocks and sea, when you were blind?

He said, 'You mustn't run away, you've got to help.' The girl said nothing, just lay staring at him with wide eyes that were the same colour as her green scarf. He wondered, for a desperate minute, if she was deaf – or mad. 'My sister, Janey,' he pleaded. 'She's alone on the beach. She's only little and she's . . .'

She swallowed. He saw the movement of her throat. She said, with what seemed tremendous effort, 'Janey's all right.' And then, as if in speaking to him she had broken through some barrier, she relaxed and smiled shyly. 'She's my friend.'

He looked at her. 'I know,' he said suddenly. 'You're the girl on the beach.'

He let her go and lay back on the grass. 'My foot hurts,' he said.

She knelt to look. His ankle was swollen like a fruit, tight inside the skin of his sock. She removed his shoe and then, very gently, peeled off the sock. She took off her green scarf, soaked it under the waterfall, and wrapped it round his ankle. The cold was soothing. She examined his face anxiously and said, after a minute, 'Can you walk on it?'

'I can try . . .'

She helped him up and he stood, leaning on her and looking back along the face of the rock. And then down at the sea. 'I can't do it,' he said.

She smiled. 'I know a better way. On the other side of the waterfall. You'll have to lean on me.'

He looked at her doubtfully. She was small, no bigger than Janey, but when she pulled his arm round her shoulder and stood steady to support him, he could feel she was strong as a little pony. Round the back of the fall, a broad shelf jutted out from the rock. Hopping, leaning on her, Tim managed to pass behind the gleaming curtain of water to the other side, where an easy, natural path snaked upwards through the battlements of rock. The cold water bandage had eased his foot considerably and, by the time they reached the heathery crown of the rock, Tim was able to limp along without support.

He began to feel he had made a fool of himself. 'It was just bad luck I twisted my ankle,' he said. ''Twasn't a difficult climb – I've done lots of climbs that are much more difficult than *that*. Why, Dad and I climbed down the big waterfall to Carlin's Cave. That's terrible dangerous. It's so dangerous I shouldn't think anyone else has ever been there ...'

There was a surprised look in her green eyes. 'I've often been,' she said simply. 'It's a bit hard, the waterfall way, though it's the quickest way home, but you can go round the headland, that's not hard at all. It doesn't take long, from the bay. Will Campbell beaches his boat there when he goes lobster fishing and sometimes Mr Smith meets him there, and they go lobster fishing together. I think it's a bit silly, really, because Mr Smith never eats lobsters, but Annie says he just catches them for sport, and for sending to his friends.'

Tim was too occupied, getting down off the rock, to pay much attention to her.

'She knew you'd hurt yourself,' Janey said. 'We were writing in the sand and then she stopped and said you were hurt.'

Tim, resting on the beach and nursing his aching foot, looked at Perdita curiously. He thought her a very odd girl. 'How'd you know?' he asked. 'I didn't call or anything.'

'I just knew,' Perdita said, hanging her head and speaking very low. 'I got this feeling ...' She stopped. She couldn't explain it. 'Annie says it's the Second Sight,' she said.

Tim stared at her blankly. He looked pale and very tired, and because this was something that always made Mr Smith laugh and cheer up when *he* was tired, Perdita said, 'She says I've got the Second Sight because I'm a witch's daughter.'

But Tim didn't laugh. He frowned. 'There's no such things as witches.'

Janey said, crossly, 'You don't *know* that, do you?' She caught her breath. 'Witches can fly. Can *you* fly, Perdita?'

Perdita hesitated. She wasn't certain. When she was alone sometimes and shut her eyes, she thought she could. She remembered the feeling but now it seemed unreal, like a dream.

'I'd like to fly,' Janey said. She stood up and spread out her arms like wings. They were sitting in the lee of the great rock, but once Janey moved out of its shelter, the wind was so strong she could almost lean against it. It blew her hair and snatched her clothes. She danced, whirling her arms, staggering against the wind. 'The wind makes you fly,' she cried. 'I'm flying now, in the wind. Is this how you fly, Perdita?'

'It's just an illusion,' Tim said.

Janey collapsed on the ground. 'I *did* fly,' she cried. 'I felt myself flying – over the land and over the sea.'

'It feels like that,' Tim explained. 'But it's an illusion, like I said. Like . . . like when you look up at a mountain and it seems to move because the clouds are going so fast.'

Janey, who had never seen mountains or clouds, could not understand this. But Perdita did. She looked thoughtful, suddenly, and then she stood up as Janey had done, and spread out her arms to the buffeting wind. She remembered what flying was like, or thought she remembered: sitting on the rock in the bay, she had flown with the gulls in the air. Now, though she tried hard, the feeling was slipping away from her. 'It's just the wind blowing,' she said.

She opened her eyes and sat down. Tim was smiling at her, and she said, rather crossly, 'I can see through walls, though, and round corners.'

'Not really,' Tim said. 'I mean scientifically speaking, that's nonsense. It's a sort of *guessing*.'

'Second Sight's knowing, not guessing.' Perdita looked obstinate. 'You don't see with your eyes.'

'I know what's happening and I can't see at all,' Janey said triumphantly. 'So I've got Second Sight, too. Only not as good as Perdita. I didn't know something had happened to you, and *she* did.'

Tim drew a deep breath. 'There's a scientific explanation for everything,' he said, and wondered what the explanation could be. 'She knew the rock is dangerous,' he said. 'She knew I'd been gone a long time . . .'

'I wasn't thinking about you. Not for *one minute*.' Perdita sat bolt upright, her green eyes bright and angry. She was angry, because, in spite of being underfed and badly dressed she was, in a way, extremely spoiled: no one in her whole life had ever contradicted or disbelieved her as Tim was doing now. There had been no one to do so, except old Annie MacLaren and she believed in witches herself.

'I've got Powers,' Perdita said. 'Annie says so. She says my mother was a witch.'

7

WHAT IS A DIAMOND?

'She was drowned in the loch, the poor, dear soul,' Annie MacLaren said. 'Such a young, pretty thing, and the poor bairn only a few weeks old and not even christened. It was the minister named her. Call her Perdita, he said. An outlandish name, I thought.'

'Pretty, though,' Mr Smith said. 'And her father?'

Sitting back in her chair and smoothing the rheumaticky knobs on her hands, Annie MacLaren looked into the fire. 'Drowned, too. He was a fisherman, his boat went down and his poor young wife never got over it. My brother found her, wandering in the bog with the baby, and we took her in. No one else would. Of course, she was a foreigner . . .'

'You mean she came from another island?' Mr Smith hid a smile: old Annie was not often in a talkative mood, and he didn't want to offend her.

'No. She was Spanish or Italian – one of those people. She'd been a waitress in Glasgow and never got used to our ways. She kept away from people and they kept away from *her*. They said,' – she gave Mr Smith a suddenly sharp look – 'they said she was a witch.'

'Kept herself to herself,' Mr Smith said. 'You don't have to be a witch to do that.'

'Maybe not. But they said she turned the milk sour. People kept their children away. Not that I listened to their talk, but she was strange, there's no doubt. Never talked, walked the hills alone . . . It was grief, my brother said, but women have lost husbands before and not acted like that.'

'A foreign girl, in a strange land?' Mr Smith said softly, but Annie, who was a little deaf, did not hear him.

'She went into the loch one night in the mist,' she said. 'People say the Lake Horse took her.'

'The Lake Horse?'

'It's a story.' The old woman spoke with some restraint, and then added, 'Though some have seen it, mind. A great horse, galloping on the water.'

'A story to frighten children.' Mr Smith laughed. 'Or to keep them away from the loch?'

'Maybe,' Annie said, very dryly. 'And maybe not. Who's to know?'

He felt her sudden antagonism: to win her back, he said, 'Anyway, you kept the child. That was good of you, Annie.'

'We'd no choice,' Annie said. 'Who else would take her? Not that I regret it. She's like my own bairn, even if she is a bit ...' She drew breath and spoke firmly. 'Whatever her mother was, or was not, the child has gifts.'

'She's sharp as a needle. Keeps her ears and eyes open. Isn't that all, Annie?'

'Not all, no. She saved my life once. And in such a way – oh, I daresay you'll not believe it.'

She spoke irritably, as if she found him unbearably foolish.

'Try me,' Mr Smith said.

'It isn't fancy.' Annie's voice held a warning and Mr Smith composed his face so that whatever she said, he wouldn't smile. 'Outside our croft, we had this big tree. One end of the washing line was tied to it. I was out one evening, taking the line down, when she came out. She'd been fast asleep only a minute before – she was only little, then, and I'd tucked her up in bed – but there she was in her nightgown, calling me. She said *Come away, come away Annie*. I ran, thinking she was frightened, and just as I got to her there was a great *crack*, and the tree fell, where I'd been standing. I picked her up and took her in, thinking it was my good luck she had had a bad dream and woken, and I asked what had frightened her. She looked up and

66

smiled and said, *I wasn't frightened, Annie, I just didn't want the old tree to hurt you.'*

The kettle hissed on the fire and a clinker dropped. Mr Smith sat silent. Of course it could be explained away, nothing easier. Old Annie would not deliberately lie, but fright could have distorted her memory – even put words into a child's mouth that had never been spoken. *I'm glad the old tree didn't hurt you, Annie.* That was the only change needed to turn the story into a simple tale of coincidence and good luck. On the other hand, the child – the little witch, he thought with a sudden grin – *was* disconcerting. She had a way of looking at you with that wide, green stare. ... It wasn't surprising that a foolish old woman should believe she had special 'powers'. He might, if he stayed here much longer on this lonely island, come to believe it himself ...

He brushed the back of his hand across his eyes. *Of course it wasn't true*. The child was sharp, as he had said to Annie, she used her wits, that was all. If she seemed strange, sometimes, it was because she was too much alone.

'She should go to school,' he said, aloud.

Annie MacLaren looked at him in surprise. 'I thought you didn't want her mixing.'

'Well ...' Mr Smith hesitated. There was something he had to tell Annie sometime, he might as well tell her now. Even if she gossiped, which was unlikely, it hardly mattered now he would soon be gone. And he had to go. He had lived on Skua for three years without anyone suspecting he had any particular purpose here. He had been safe, but he was no longer as safe as he had been. The islanders were simple, unsuspicious people, but there were other people not so simple. Mr Smith did not underestimate the police. Once their attention had been drawn to Skua by Mr Jones's foolish behaviour, they would be curious. They might even be curious about Mr Smith, that quiet, country gentleman living a retired life beside a loch ...

'I shall be leaving, Annie,' Mr Smith said. 'Quite soon. And when I go, I want you to send her to school.'

He looked at the old woman. The things that family man, Mr Jones, had said, had pricked his rather sluggish conscience. 'She should have a proper chance, Annie,' he said. 'She's under-sized for her age, she should have more milk and orange juice and she shouldn't run wild. But school's the main thing.' He felt, suddenly, generous and full of sentiment. 'I'll see you're all right, Annie, there'll be money, don't worry about that. Just see she gets to school and has a chance to grow up like other children. Not too full of superstitious ideas – not thinking she's different . . .'

'Annie says I'm different,' Perdita said. It was all she would say. She had gone sullen and obstinate with Tim, the way Janey did sometimes, he thought. *Girls.* They were all the same. Whenever you disagreed with them and tried to put them right, they were inclined to get cross and sulk.

The swelling in his foot had subsided a little, but it still ached enough to make him feel irritable and moody. He sat deliber-ately apart and ate sandwiches while Perdita and Janey whis-pered and giggled together. Perdita was showing Janey something that she was wearing round her neck on a piece of string. She had been wearing it when she found him, he re-membered, but he had not noticed it since: perhaps she had tucked it inside the neck of her dress.

'What is it?' he asked, idly interested.

Perdita turned, pulling away from Janey and clutching her hand across her flat little chest.

'It's a lucky stone she's got,' Janey said.

'Show me,' he coaxed Perdita, less because he really wanted to see it than because he felt he had been unkind: witches were nonsense, of course, but it had been mean to laugh at her.

But she shook her head, her mouth pursed and stubborn. ''Twon't stay lucky, if I show you.'

'You showed Janey.'

Perdita frowned. Showing Janey the stone was all right. Mr Jones had talked about *showing* people: he had said nothing about letting someone *feel* it.

Tim edged nearer, a glint in his eye. 'Please ...' he said, giving her a chance, but when she shook her head again, he laughed and grabbed at her. He had only meant to tease, not to force her to show her secret, but, taken by surprise, she over-balanced and thrust both hands behind her to steady herself.

Netted like a lobster float, but in thinner string, the lucky stone winked and flashed on her chest. Tim stared at it in wonder. There might be doubt about his ruby, but there was none about *this*. It was like the central stone in his mother's engagement ring, but much larger, much brighter ...

Perdita was astonished. She was not used to boys who teased and grabbed her. Alistair Campbell might throw a stone, but he was too scared to lay a finger on her: he would be afraid she might put a spell on him.

But this boy wasn't afraid. There was only awestruck wonder in his face as he stared at the stone. 'It's a *diamond*,' he said in a high, squeaky voice.

Perdita picked the stone up from her chest and squinted down at it. 'What's a diamond?' she asked.

'What's a ...'

Tim transferred his gaze to her face, which was innocently inquiring.

'Don't you *know*?' It seemed incredible to him, though of course it wasn't really: Annie MacLaren had no engagement ring, and so the word had never entered Perdita's vocabulary.

'Well ...' Tim expelled his breath slowly. 'A diamond's a ... a ... valuable thing. Like emeralds or rubies or gold. It's ... well ... treasure ...'

Perdita's expression remained puzzled.

Tim sighed. 'You've heard about treasure trove, haven't you? I mean, you must have read about it in books?'

'She can't read,' Janey said.

'Can't . . . oh, I see.' Although this seemed just as extra-ordinary as not knowing what a diamond was, Tim nodded casually, the way his father did when he had accepted a point in an argument: he thought Perdita must have been terribly shamed by this revelation and he did not want to embarrass her further. After all, it was only babies or very stupid people who couldn't read . . .

He spoke to her slowly, as if she were indeed very stupid.

'Do you know what "valuable" means?'

'Worth a lot of money.' Perdita touched her stone. 'Is this worth a lot of money, then?' She thought a minute, and then smiled. 'I can give it to Annie for her old age. She's always worrying about that. She says all she wants is a bit of peace and comfort. Would this be enough to buy her a bit of peace and comfort?'

'I should think so,' Tim said. But he was not really interested in Annie. Something else was puzzling – and exciting – him. She must have picked up this diamond somewhere. Suppose she had found it in the cave where he had found his ruby – suppose his ruby *was* a ruby, after all – suppose it *was* a smuggler's cave . . .

'Where'd you find it?' he demanded. And then, though anything else seemed unlikely, '*Did* you find it?'

Perdita shook her head slowly. *A piece of glass worth a king's ransom.* That's what Mr Jones had said. 'Mr Jones said it was a piece of glass,' she said, and paused. 'What's a king's ransom?' she asked.

'Just another way of saying a lot of money. D'you mean someone *gave* it to you?'

Perdita nodded. 'He said he'd got plenty more, so I don't suppose it mattered giving me one.' She laughed suddenly. '*That's* what he had in the box! I thought it was toffees!'

Tim noticed nothing. It was Janey who made the connexion. Since she could not look at people's faces while they talked, she always listened very closely to what they said. 'Was it our Mr Jones who gave you the stone, then? We call him Toffee Papers.'

She said absently, 'He did eat a lot of toffees and dropped the paper about. Annie was cross because of the mess. But I call him Frog Face.'

'He has got a face like a frog,' Tim said. 'Sort of bulgy and flat at the same time.' It struck him that this was not altogether polite, although Perdita had mentioned it first. 'Sorry,' he muttered.

'Why?' Perdita asked.

'Well. It's a bit rude, my saying that, when he's a friend of yours.'

'Oh, he's not a friend of *mine*,' Perdita said cheerfully. 'I just met him once, that's all.'

Tim's eyes grew round. This was becoming more and more extraordinary. A witch's daughter who wore a diamond round her neck – a diamond given her by Mr Jones, whom she had only met once! And yet he was sure she wasn't lying.

'Where'd you meet him?' he asked abruptly.

Perdita said nothing. She had already said too much, she suddenly realized. Mr Smith did not want talk about his visitor. She had promised Annie. She hung her head and began to draw letters in the sand, pretending she had not heard Tim's question.

But he thought he knew the answer to it. He had found a stone on the beach, which looked like a ruby. Suppose there were others – not necessarily a smuggler's treasure trove, but a box of jewels, perhaps, washed ashore from a wrecked ship. Suppose Toffee Papers had found it and Perdita had seen him, and he had given her the diamond. Why? Why would he do that? Perhaps – Tim began to feel very excited – perhaps because he didn't want to hand the jewels over to the police and it was a sort of bribe . . .

'Did he tell you to keep it secret?' he asked.

Perdita said nothing.

'Did he find it on the beach?' Tim went on. 'Did he . . .'

But Perdita stood up. 'I'm going now,' she said.

'Are you going home?' Janey asked. 'Where do you live?'

But Perdita did not answer, only ducked her head and ran fast across the sand. They watched her disappear in the dunes and then appear again, climbing up the cropped turf to the dry-stone wall.

'You shouldn't have kept on asking things,' Janey said. 'She doesn't like it.'

'You don't find out things if you don't ask,' Tim said.

'That'll be Annie MacLaren's foster daughter,' Mrs Tarbutt said. 'Lives up at Luinpool. Annie MacLaren's housekeeper to Mr Smith. I'm surprised she spoke to you. She's a shy creature.'

'Wild,' Mr Tarbutt said and grinned at the children, sitting at the table in the hotel kitchen and eating their tea. 'You ought to watch out, young Tim,' he said solemnly. 'The children round here fight shy of her. They say she's a witch.'

'Now, Father . . .' Mrs Tarbutt gave him a reproachful look. 'Fancy filling them up with that nonsense.' She said, to Tim, 'They're not very sociable, up at Luinpool. The little lass doesn't mix with other children. So they think she's strange.'

'That's all, is it?' Mr Tarbutt winked at Tim. 'Mrs Tarbutt's town bred. She comes from Edinburgh.'

'I don't see what that's got to do with it,' Mrs Tarbutt said primly.

'Town people only believe what they see under their noses,' Mr Tarbutt said. 'No respect for the supernatural.'

'Certainly I haven't any,' Mrs Tarbutt said, with a little toss of her head and a smile for her husband, whose teasing she enjoyed. 'I've got better things to think about.' Then the smile left her face and she looked suddenly worried. 'Such as Mr Jones. Here it is, tea time and no sign of him – no sign since last night.'

Mr Tarbutt smiled. 'He's all right. I told you not to worry. He probably went off early this morning.'

Mrs Tarbutt looked thoughtful. 'His bed was mussed up, as if he'd slept in it, but, d'you know, I wondered if he *had*? His washbasin was tidy and he usually makes a fine old mess, shaving in the morning.'

'If he went off early, he wouldn't bother to shave,' Mr Tarbutt said. 'I've got an idea he may have gone shooting with Campbell. He was saying he thought he'd be going one day soon, after deer. Maybe he offered to take Mr Jones – they were thick last night, in the bar.'

'It's odd he didn't tell us though, isn't it?' Mrs Tarbutt said.

'Odd. But not odd enough to worry. He'll turn up before dark, I daresay.' Mr Tarbutt grinned broadly. 'Unless the fairies have taken him,' he said.

8

WRECKED SHIPS AND TREASURE

'What are you doing, Tim?' Janey asked.

'Thinking.'

'Can I look at your stones, then?'

'If you want to.'

Janey picked up the box clumsily, and spilled the stones on the floor.

'Look what you've done,' Tim said crossly. 'Interrupting me. . . . Pick them up, every one.'

Janey knelt and swept her hands over the floor, feeling for the stones. She counted them into the box in a low, droning voice. 'Twenty-nine,' she said. She sat back on her heels and looked puzzled. 'Funny – there's twenty-nine and there should be twenty-nine altogether . . .'

'What's funny, then?'

'Well, the last one you got isn't here.'

'The ruby one?' Tim looked at the box. 'Here it is, silly.' He picked up the red stone and gave it to Janey. She felt it carefully, turning it in her fingers and stroking the surface. 'This isn't it,' she said.

''Course it is,' Tim said. 'Don't interrupt me when I'm thinking.'

In fact he wasn't thinking, so much as dreaming – about Perdita's diamond and his ruby, and wrecked ships and treasure . . .

Janey was frowning. 'It isn't the same, though. The other one had more – more *sides*, and there was a sort of gritty patch . . .'

Tim took the stone from her. It looked the same – or it had looked the same until now. Now, he wasn't sure whether it

74

looked different or whether he knew it must be different because Janey had said so. There didn't seem to be so much colour in it, so much life and fire. 'It looks just like red glass,' he whispered.

'The burglar stole it,' Janey said. 'He came in and stole it and changed it for *this* one. This is a new one. I never saw it before.'

She would be right about that, Tim knew. She never made a mistake about things she had felt carefully, and got to know. His heart jumped in his throat. Janey never made a mistake about what she heard, either . . .

He was terrified. 'Janey,' he whispered. 'Janey – perhaps there was a burglar here last night, after all . . .'

'I told you there was, didn't I?' Janey said in an irritated voice.

'Ssh,' Tim said. He slipped off the bed, where he had been sitting to think, and rest his foot, and went to close the bedroom door.

'I wasn't awake enough to be scared, really,' Janey said. 'But I heard someone breathing . . .'

There was a catch in her voice. Tim knelt and put his arm round her shoulders.

'We ought to tell Mr Tarbutt,' she said.

'You did tell him last night. He didn't believe you.'

'About the ruby, I mean. It must have been a ruby, or the burglar wouldn't have stolen it, would he? So if you tell Mr Tarbutt, he'll know there was a burglar and he'll tell the police and they'll catch him and put him in prison. Then you'll get the ruby back and we'll sell it and we'll all be rich for ever and ever . . .'

Janey gave a happy little sigh, as if she had just finished telling herself a lovely story.

And that's what it would sound like to Mr Tarbutt, Tim thought. A lovely story. 'He wouldn't believe a word of it,' he said.

'Why ever not?' Janey asked. 'You just show him the stone and tell him someone stole yours. It's proof.'

'No,' Tim said. 'Or it's only proof for *us*. I mean, we know it's different, but Mr Tarbutt won't know.'

'We'll tell him, then,' Janey said confidently.

Tim said nothing. He believed the stone was different, because Janey had said it was, but Mr Tarbutt would never understand how Janey could be so sure. He didn't know Janey. He didn't know that she would remember the shape of something she had seen with her fingers better than an ordinary person who had only used his eyes. Only their mother and father would understand that.

'We'd best not say anything till we see Dad,' he said. 'Though I don't suppose he'll believe it either. I mean, he'll believe in the burglar, all right, once his memory comes back, and he'll believe he took my stone, but he'll think it was just some sort of mistake . . .'

'What sort of mistake?'

Tim sighed. 'Oh, I dunno. But you know what Dad *is*. He'll find out some sort of reason . . . he *saw* the ruby, you see, and he didn't believe it was one.'

He got up and went to the window. He stood, staring out. In his mind, he could hear his father's calm, reasonable voice, talking and talking. *My dear Tim, even if it was a ruby, which I don't happen to believe, why should anyone steal it? After all, no one knew you had it, did they?*

Suddenly Tim's heart gave a leap, like a fish jumping in his throat. Mr Smith had known. He had said it wasn't a ruby, but if he was a crook, he would have said that anyway, wouldn't he? So that he would have time to find a piece of glass that looked just like it before he came to the hotel, creeping in to steal like a thief in the night. . . . But how could he have got in? The window had been bolted and no one had come into the hotel by the door. At least, Toffee Papers had been sure no one had. He and Mr Campbell had been sitting in the bar all the time. Mr Campbell. Was it the same Mr Campbell Mr Smith knew, the one who lived in the tent on the beach? Of course Campbell was as common a name in Scotland as Smith was in England. But suppose it *was* the same man. Suppose Mr Smith had told him about the ruby and Mr Campbell had told Toffee Papers . . .

'He stole my stone,' Tim said loudly. 'Toffee Papers stole my stone, because he didn't want anyone to know there was treasure on the beach. And when Dad came in and caught him, he knocked him down.' He clenched his fists. 'He ought to be put in prison.'

'How do you know he found the treasure on the beach?' Janey asked.

Something in the calm way she spoke might have made Tim doubtful if he had not been so absorbed in his own thoughts. 'Well, because Perdita must've met him on the beach and that was when he gave her the diamond.'

'She didn't meet him on the beach,' Janey said. 'He was up at her house. She said Annie was cross because of the mess he made with the toffee papers. Don't you remember?'

Now she had told him, he did. He whistled slowly through his teeth. 'So they *must* both be in it, him and Mr Smith. And Mr Campbell too. They all found some buried treasure or something, and they want to keep it quiet . . .'

Oh, Tim, Tim . . . He could hear his father's voice and his gently amused laugh, as clearly as if he had been in the room. *Don't let your imagination run away with you. That sort of thing only happens in books.*

'Do you think he's still there?' Janey asked.

'Who's still where?'

'Toffee Papers. Mr Jones. Mrs Tarbutt said she didn't know where he was. Well, he might be up at Perdita's house.'

'Could be.' Tim spoke rather coldly, because he should have thought of this for himself. 'If it *was* him, knocked Dad down, he'd have run away because he'd be afraid Dad would tell the police about him. So I suppose he might have gone to – to this place, whatever it's called.'

'Luinpool,' Janey said patiently. 'Don't you ever listen?'

'I did listen,' Tim said, 'but I was busy *thinking*. And if you'll kindly keep quiet, I'm going to think *now*.'

He frowned and made deep, sighing noises to help the process. *I expect there is some perfectly simple explanation*, his father would say. And by *simple* he would mean that it must have nothing to do with smuggler's caves or buried treasure. What his father would say – what would his father say? Tim frowned more fiercely as he tried to guess what would be the – extraordinarily dull, he thought – processes of his father's mind. His father would say, he realized, that neither the ruby, nor Perdita's diamond, were real. *Too romantic an imagination, old chap.* And he would ruffle his son's hair with a sigh: imagination was not a quality Mr Hoggart thought highly of.

'But they *were* real, weren't they?' Tim said aloud.

He stood, biting the side of his thumb nail, and feeling confused. *Evidence* – he could hear Mr Hoggart saying it – *where is your evidence?* So far he had only got Janey's word that there had been a burglar. And, though his father must have seen him and would tell the police as soon as he got better and remembered, he hadn't told them yet, had he? Suppose he never did remember? Suppose he had lost his memory completely as a result of that bang on the head? Would he believe Janey's story then? Would anyone? Of course they wouldn't. Unless . . .

He whirled round. 'Janey,' he said in a hoarse whisper, 'Janey – I know what we'll do.'

9

THE HEROIC BEHAVIOUR OF
MR JONES

THE witch's daughter lay on the rag rug in front of the range fire, her face to the ground. She was crying. She could hardly remember crying before – at least, not for years and years. 'Witch's can't cry, it's a known fact,' Mr Smith had once said when she had fallen in the yard and cut her lip on a stone. And to please him, she had sat dry-eyed on the kitchen table while he dabbed at the cut with disinfectant – clumsily because, unlike Mr Jones, he was not a family man.

But now Mr Smith was going away. Annie had told her, and Perdita had been dry-eyed while she listened, staring at Annie with wide, unbelieving eyes. She had said nothing until Annie had gone out to feed the hens, and then the tears had burst out, gushing up like a fountain. She cried until she felt empty and weak. Then she rolled over and blinked her swollen eyes at the fire. She lay like that until she heard Annie at the back door, stamping the yard mud from her boots. Perdita got up and ran out of the kitchen, into the hall and up the stairs.

Mr Smith was out. The old house breathed and creaked with the wind. Perdita stood at the end of the long corridor at the top of the stairs and listened to the familiar sounds. Familiar – but there was something different too. The plumbing clanged as Annie turned a tap on downstairs, but it wasn't that. It was a new creak, a questioning little whine, like a door hinge. Perdita tiptoed along the corridor and saw that one of the locked rooms was open: the dark wood of the solid door was edged with light. She stood outside it, listening. The hinge creaked and the door blew shut. Then a breathy sigh, and it opened again just that little, lighted crack, as if the wind had sucked it inwards. Gently, Perdita put her hand on the door and pushed it.

It opened wide, on to a large, light room that was empty except for a camp bed with some blankets tumbled on it, and an open suitcase in the corner. The floor was a mess of mouse dirts and dust; the sunlight, falling through the dirty window, showed up a filmy pattern of cobwebs. Perdita crept across the floor to the window, which looked out on to the loch. The water was rippling with the wind and the wind pump was rattling round like a child's paper windmill. Across the loch, the sun had gone behind the hills, turning them into sombre shadows, etched with dazzling light.

Perdita blinked her eyes, which felt hot and sore. She turned from the window and looked at the suitcase.

There was nothing remarkable about it. Just an old suitcase with a pair of shoes that needed mending, a few, crumpled magazines, newspapers. . . . Newspapers. Suddenly interested, Perdita squatted down to see if there was anything she could read. But none of the letters seemed much like the wobbly ones Janey had drawn in the sand.

She began to turn the newspapers over. The paper felt brittle, like dry leaves, and smelt musty. She wrinkled her nose and was about to shut the case, when a picture caught her eye. A photograph. There was no mistaking that flat, froggy face. It was Mr Jones's photograph, staring up at her from the front page.

There was some print underneath, in blacker type than the rest of the lettering, and easier to read. Mr. That was Mister. She muttered to herself. J should be the beginning of the next word, then. J for Janey and for Jam and for Jones. But it wasn't. The first letter of the next word was a P.

P for Perdita. She breathed deeply, concentrating hard, and the letters stopped being just squiggles on the page and became meaningful. P for Perdita. R for Rat. A for Apple. T for Tomato. Then another T. P – she said the sound to herself. R – rolling the R. A. T.T. P R A T T. Mr Pratt.

Exhausted, she sat back on her heels, smiling. She had read a printed word. For a moment that was all it meant to her: a small triumph, the first step on the way to the school on Trull. Then puzzlement set in. Why should Mr Jones have a different name in the newspaper? She stared hard at the smaller print under the headline, but it told her nothing. Her mouth set in temper and she tore the page out, crumpling it in her hand to throw it away. Then, almost at once, her expression changed. Tim could read. He and Janey knew Mr Jones too. She smoothed the wrinkled page on the floor, folded it, and tucked it inside the neck of her dress.

At the hotel in Skuaphort, the telephone began to ring. Mr Tarbutt came out of the bar and went to answer it. Mrs Hoggart began to talk at the other end, her voice quick and excited. 'Can't hear you. Bad line,' Mr Tarbutt said.

The voice at the other end slowed down.

Mr Tarbutt listened, scratching his head with his free hand in a bewildered fashion. 'I don't quite understand. Are you sure your husband is quite ...' he began, and then, hastily, 'Oh, no, Mrs Hoggart, of course I believe you, it's just that. ... No, he's not here, we've not seen him all day, and, as a matter of fact my wife was quite worried but if what you say is ...' He cleared his throat loudly. 'I mean, it looks as if he may have skipped off to avoid trouble. ... What. ... Oh, the children are fine, just had their tea. ... Yes, of course you can speak to Tim.'

He put the receiver down and went to the foot of the stairs. He called Tim and waited. When there was no answer, he ran up the stairs and opened the bedroom door. A piece of paper blew off the dressing-table in the draught. Mr Tarbutt stooped for it, frowned, and went heavily down the stairs. He picked up the receiver and said, reluctantly, 'I'm afraid they're not here. Tim left a note. It just says they'll be back before dark.'

He listened to Mrs Hoggart's voice, which had begun to quack in a loud, alarmed way. Then he gave a brief, involuntary smile.

'Oh, please don't worry, Mrs Hoggart. I'm sure he is not a dangerous criminal. Even if he did attack your husband, I can't believe he'd harm the children, even if he ran into them, which isn't likely. Tim won't have gone far, not with the little lass. . . . Yes, of course, I'll go out and look for them at once. . . . No. No, Mrs Hoggart, I'm afraid there isn't a police station here.'

A man had appeared in the doorway of the hotel. He stood there, his hands in his pockets, his face expressionless. Mr Tarbutt promised that he would telephone as soon as he had found the children. Then he put the receiver down and the man in the doorway spoke. 'Police station?' Mr Smith said. 'Who wants a policeman on Skua?'

'We ought to have told a policeman,' Janey said.

'What policeman? There isn't even a doctor on Skua. And who'd believe us, anyway? No one would listen, Janey. Not without evidence. We've got to get evidence first.'

'Are you going to ask Mr Jones for your ruby back? Are we going to see Perdita, at Luinpool?'

'Well . . .' Tim hesitated. That had, in fact, been his first indignant reaction: to walk up to Luinpool and confront Mr Jones. Then doubt had set in. Suppose he was wrong, after all. Suppose there was some 'perfectly simple explanation' which had, so far, eluded him? What a fool he would look! Even if someone had knocked his father down, there was no proof it was Toffee Papers. At least, he had no proof. And if he was right – well, if he was right, to go up to Luinpool might be dangerous!

'I think it's better to go to the cave first,' he said. 'If I found the ruby there, I expect that's where Mr Jones found the treasure. So there might be another one.' He breathed quickly, with excitement. 'If we could find another ruby, Janey, then they'd have to believe us.'

'But it's a long way to Carlin's Cave,' Janey protested. 'You and Dad went by car.'

'It's only a long way by road. Not if we go round by the headland.'

If they could go round by the headland. *If* Perdita was right about the path . . .

'How far is it?' Janey asked.

'A bit beyond the bay.' Tim looked at his sister. She was a good walker, but it was already late in the day and she would soon be tired. 'I should have left you behind,' he said. 'I *told* you to stay behind . . .'

'I wouldn't though, would I?' Janey said, smiling to herself.

Tim gave a little sigh. 'No, you wouldn't. Well, you mustn't grumble, then.'

Janey showed no sign of grumbling. She walked stoutly beside Tim who still limped a little, and held on to the sleeve of his wind-cheater for guidance. 'We're nearly at the bay now,' she said.

'How d'you know?' Tim said, surprised.

'We're out of the peaty bog. It's grassy here, sort of springy. Then you get to the stone wall and over the wall there's the up and down sandy part with the prickly grasses.'

'The dunes,' Tim said. 'I'll carry you through the dunes, if you like.'

'No. I don't mind. It tells me where I am.'

They had reached the bay and were crossing the sand towards the headland when Perdita saw them. She was walking the ridge of Ben Luin. She looked down at Skuaphort and saw Mr Smith's white Jaguar drive away from the hotel and up the stony road. Then she looked down at the bay and saw Tim and Janey. She called out, but the wind was strong and tossed her voice away like a bird cry. She ran down off the ridge, so fast that her teeth jolted. The wind was very strong now, and the sky was sullen over the sea.

There was a path round the headland, a narrow path, a goat track. It wound up the cliff a little, through heather, and then descended on the seaward side, a tiny ledge on the sheer cliff face. It was safe enough as long as you didn't look down and turn giddy. Tim looked down once: beneath him, the sea boiled over rocks that were sharp and pointed like – like dragon's teeth, he thought. He had to stop. Behind him, holding on to his wind-cheater, Janey had to stop too. 'What's the matter? Have we got there?'

'No.' Tim swallowed. There was no point in telling her about that terrible drop. 'It's just my foot aching,' he said, and forced himself on again.

The precipitous part was mercifully short. Once round the point of the headland – the Point of Caves – the path went a little inland, through two walls of rock, as if here the cliff had split open at some time. The rocky walls were high above them: all Tim could see when he looked up, was the purplish, menacing sky. *If it rains*, he thought, *it'll be slippery going back*, and the thought made his stomach churn, as if he had eaten too much ice-cream. He wasn't afraid for himself, he thought, but for Janey. *She* wasn't frightened, of course. Whenever he stopped, she prodded him in the back and said, 'Hurry up, lazy. I want to get to the cave.'

From this approach the cave and the little beach looked quite different from when Tim and his father had come down the side of the torrent. Tim could see, what he had not noticed then, that beyond the rocks was a small, natural harbour. A boat was moored there, rocking among the gingery seaweed. An outboard motor was propped up on the stern and the bottom of the boat was full of fishing tackle and lobster pots.

'That's Mr Campbell's boat,' Perdita said, as she came panting up to join them.

They sat on the shingle beach and looked at Mr Jones's picture in the newspaper. Toffee Papers, Frog Face, Mr Jones. Pratt was the name the newspaper used. And Mr Pratt – who was fifty-two, the newspaper said, and had two little girls –

was not a burglar, or, indeed, a criminal of any kind. He was an assistant in a big jeweller's shop in the West End of London, and an extremely brave man. When the shop had been raided by a gang late one winter afternoon, Mr Pratt, who had stayed after closing time to finish stock-taking, had behaved with great courage. Hearing a noise in the shop, he had telephoned the police from the back office, and then fearing they would not arrive in time, he had attempted to prevent the thieves making a get-away. It was gallant but useless: when the police reached the shop they found the thieves gone, and poor Mr Pratt gagged and blindfolded and trussed up like a chicken ready for the oven. He had been badly hurt, severely bruised and cut about the face, and it was some time before he recovered sufficiently to make a statement. The odds had been terribly against him: there had been seven or eight men, though he could only describe one. 'It all happened so suddenly,' he said. The man he had seen was of medium height, not fat, not thin: he wore a hat and a raincoat and Mr Pratt had thought his eyes were brown, but he couldn't be sure.

Tim frowned down at the newspaper. 'Seems to me,' he said, 'that *that* could be a description of just about anybody. I mean – if you *had* to describe somebody, but didn't want anyone to know who it was, that's just the sort of description you'd give.'

He paused. 'Perhaps he just isn't a very noticing sort of person,' he said. 'Mum says there are a lot of people who don't really notice what other people look like. She notices. She's got a good memory for faces.' He remembered something, suddenly. 'She remembered *his* face, you know. She told me she thought she'd seen him somewhere before. I suppose she'd seen his picture in the paper . . .'

He thought a minute. 'I wonder how long ago this happened. There isn't any date . . .'

'Three years, just about,' said a voice behind them.

10

UNEXPECTED EVIDENCE

IT was Toffee Papers. The sea boomed so loudly round the Point of Caves, that even Janey had not heard him come. He bent down and removed the piece of newspaper from Tim's limp fingers.

'Not a bad likeness,' he said, regarding it critically. 'Not bad at all.' His eyes bulged like pale, boiled sweets as he sat on a rock and looked at the three children. 'National hero, that's what I was. A national hero . . .'

He took a toothpick out of his waistcoat pocket and began to dig between his yellow front teeth.

'*Mr Pratt?*' Tim said.

He snapped the toothpick between his plump fingers and finished the job with his tongue. 'Being a hero can be an embarrassment. Notoriety. Begging letters. So what do you do? You change your name. You get used to the new one and it don't seem worth changing back.' He looked at the newspaper story, grinned, and handed it back to Tim. 'Where'd you find it?'

'Mr Smith's suitcase,' Perdita said.

He looked at her. 'Thought you didn't mix with other kiddies. Smithie was wrong about that, wasn't he? Poor old Smithie.' He sighed. 'It's like him to keep that cutting. He's the kind of man who's proud of his old friends.'

'What happened to the thieves?' Tim asked. He felt very confused.

Mr Jones – or Pratt – took a toffee out of his jacket pocket. He unwrapped it, popped it in his mouth, and said, 'Oh, pardon *me*. Manners!' He abstracted three more toffees from his pocket and tossed them over to the children. '*Now*. The thieves. The gentlemen of fortune. They got away with it, young man. Deserved to, in my opinion. It was a clever job, a clever job. They weren't ordinary criminals, you know, not regulars. One job and clean away. That's the way to do it.'

'What happened to the jewels?' Tim was hypnotized by Toffee Papers' broad, rhythmically chewing jaw.

'Never seen again. Of course the market was watched, but not a sign! That's the way to be successful, of course. Sit on the loot, don't spend it – or only spend it carefully, bit by bit. If you start spending money like water it attracts attention. That's the way fools get caught. These weren't fools, you know, these were clever men.'

'I shouldn't have thought you'd have thought so,' Tim could not help saying. 'After what they did to you.'

Toffee Papers looked faintly startled and then laughed. 'Oh, they rough-housed me a bit. But I don't bear any malice now.' He leaned forward, his fat hands on his fat knees. 'I was angry at first – mad! Then, after a bit, I got to thinking. What harm had they done, after all? Pinched a lot of stuff that was no real use to anyone. You can't eat diamonds – nor warm yourself by them, neither. No one lost anything, really, except the insurance company, and they could afford it. No – I thought it over, and the months went by and they didn't get caught and I began to think – well – good luck to them! What are most people's lives like, in the end? A treadmill. You work so you can eat, you eat so you can work. Round and round like mice in a cage.' He began to get excited, waving his fists in the air. 'Here were some men, I said to myself, who'd had the courage to break out. Family men, perhaps, anxious for their children's future. But having the sense to wait. Bide their time, go on with their nine to five jobs, mowing the lawn Sundays. Then, when the hue and cry's over' – he snapped his fingers – 'OUT. Out and away . . .'

Tim was fascinated. 'But stealing's *wrong*,' he blurted out.

Toffee Papers mopped his forehead with a large, red handkerchief. He looked shaken, as if he had surprised himself by his own eloquence. Tucking his handkerchief back in his pocket, he suddenly grinned. 'You're right, boy, I'm glad to see your Dad has brought you up properly. How *is* your poor father, by the way?'

Tim hesitated. What was he to think? Then Toffee Papers turned and spoke to a man who had come round the cliff path and was standing, looking down at them. 'Campbell,' Toffee Papers called. 'Campbell – we've got company.'

Slowly, Mr Will Campbell came down over the rocks. Toffee Papers turned to the children. 'What are you doing here, by the way?' he asked, in a friendly voice.

'Looking for rubies,' Janey said. 'For evidence . . .'

Tim said quickly, 'I found a piece of stone that I thought looked like a ruby. But I – I lost it. So I came to look for another one.'

'Beachcombing, eh?' Toffee Papers said. 'Oh – you find all sorts of things, beachcombing. When I was a lad, we used to spend our holidays at Herne Bay and one day I found – what do you think? Six half crowns and a florin.'

Mr Campbell stood a little way away. 'Tide's on the turn,' he said.

'Oh – there's time,' Toffee Papers said. 'Time to help these young folk look for rubies!' He stood up, smiling and rubbing his hands together. 'You know – there might be something in the cave. Washed up by a high tide. Have you looked in the cave?'

'Only a little way. It's dark.' Tim spoke doubtfully. It all seemed so innocent. Toffee Papers, smiling and smiling in that cheerful, enthusiastic way, just like a boy. Innocent – but somehow not ordinary . . .

'Dark, is it?' Toffee Papers was rubbing the palm of his hand over his chin as if wondering whether he had shaved properly. 'We've got a torch, I expect. I have, anyway. You got a torch, Campbell?'

Mr Campbell nodded. He was watching Toffee Papers. There was an uneasy expression on his face.

Suddenly Janey clapped her hands together. 'Let's go in the cave,' she said. 'Oh, *please* let's go in the cave. I never thought I'd be able to. Tim said it was dangerous to get here, even for people who could see . . .'

Toffee Papers looked at her. Then he spoke very gently. 'All right, young lady. It won't be dangerous, not with Campbell here, and me. No harm'll come to you.' He looked at Campbell and spoke with an odd, meaning emphasis. 'No harm at all, I promise.'

Campbell shrugged his shoulders. Toffee Papers bent to take Janey's hand. He said, to Perdita, 'Take her other hand, you with the fancy name. It's rough going.'

Tim watched them enter the mouth of the cave. He felt a queer uneasiness he could not place or name. But what was wrong? What could be wrong? Toffee Papers, it appeared, was not a burglar after all. He was a fat, jolly, uncle-ish man who used to go beachcombing at Herne Bay and who did not mind sparing a little time from his fishing trip with Mr Campbell to amuse three children he had met on the beach. There was nothing sinister about him. There was the stone he had given Perdita, but that wasn't sinister, on its own. He was the sort of man who enjoyed giving children presents. If the stone really was a diamond, it was pretty odd, of course, but Tim could not be sure it was a diamond. The only thing that was really strange, when you came down to it, was his leaving the hotel before breakfast this morning without telling Mrs Tarbutt where he was going. But that was impolite, rather than sinister . . .

'Coming?' Mr Campbell said. In a half dream, Tim rose from his squatting position on the beach, and followed him into the cave. Almost at once, he forgot his doubts and fears in the excitement of discovery. The cave went back, deep into the rock. From the central cavern – which was as far as he had been with his father – several high arches led off, black as the mouths of railway tunnels. Down one of these tunnels, which had high, dark walls and a smooth, sandy floor, Tim could see the light of Toffee Papers' torch flickering. He heard Janey shouting and then her shrill, delighted laughter as the echo of her voice boomed back to her, and then Toffee Papers' exuberant boyish shout, and *his* laughter. Mr Campbell had a hurricane lamp and its light danced and swayed up the tunnel, sliding its yellow circle over the walls which seemed to be made of black columns, fitting closely together and looking in places rather like the pipes of a giant organ. The tunnel twisted and turned, other tunnels led off it and, after a little, Tim found he could not remember which one they were exploring: when he looked back, he could see only black darkness.

'Careful, now,' Mr Campbell said, swinging his lantern, and Tim saw they had come to a crack on the rock. Down – a long way down – there was water running, not booming like the sea, but rushing and gurgling like a narrow, fast river. They crossed this ravine by a ledge at the side of the tunnel which then wound upwards, up a sort of rough, natural stairway, and came into another cavern where the floor was not sandy, but made of stone. Examining it, Tim found it was the same columnar construction as the walls, only the columns were broken off, producing an effect rather like a tessellated pavement.

At the far side of this cavern, Janey and Perdita were sitting on a slightly taller column and singing, 'Life is butter, butter melon . . .' 'How does it go on?' Janey asked.

'Life is butter, butter, melon, melon, cauliflower . . .' Toffee Papers sang, broadly grinning. 'Sing it over and over,' he said, 'and you'll find it doesn't mean quite what you thought at first.'

Seeing Tim and Mr Campbell, he came over to them, leaving the girls singing. He was mopping his face, which had suddenly gone unsmiling and thoughtful, with his handkerchief.

'Not a bad place, is it?' he said. 'Dry, safe, bit of natural light.'

Mr Campbell blew out his hurricane lamp and Tim saw this was true: a faint blue-ish light filtered down from somewhere up aloft, turning the cavern into a mysterious, exciting place. The columnar walls were smooth, but they were dry and not too smooth to climb: while Janey sat, singing on her rock, with Toffee Papers beating time beside her, Tim and Perdita explored, making their way upwards along an intricate series of ledges and precarious hand-holds, until they were some thirty feet above the floor of the cave and could see the source of the light, a high, narrow chimney in the roof. Not only light came from it. As they had climbed higher and higher, they had heard a low, musical roar which grew louder and louder. Now it seemed to fill the roof of the cave.

'Perhaps it comes out under the waterfall,' Perdita said.

'I wonder if you can get up.' Tim ranged his eye over the roof of the cave, but there was nothing there to hang on to. Except, perhaps, for a bat . . .

He looked down. He could see the top of Janey's head. He couldn't hear her singing, because of the noise, but he could see her hand, beating time. There was no sign of Toffee Papers or Mr Campbell, but he supposed they were hidden from his view, under an over-hang. 'We'd better go,' he said. 'If they want to go fishing . . .'

'It's much too rough for fishing,' Perdita said.

'Well – they were going somewhere in the boat, weren't they? Mr Campbell said the tide was on the turn.'

'Perhaps they're going to Trull,' Perdita said.

'What's Trull?'

'The island, of course. Just across the water from the Point. The island of Trull.'

Perdita looked as surprised as Tim might have done, if some-one had asked him what London was.

'What do they want to go there for?'

'There's a fine, big school on Trull,' Perdita said longingly.

Tim laughed. 'I don't suppose they want to go to school.'

She shrugged her shoulders. 'Perhaps Mr Jones wants to catch an aeroplane. Perhaps he's suddenly made up his mind to go to South America. He told Mr Smith he was thinking of going there.' And then, as if there was nothing at all unusual in Mr Jones making a sudden decision to fly across the world – and, indeed, Perdita would not see anything surprising in it, as she did not know where South America was – she added, 'I think I'll go down and play with Janey, now.'

She began to climb down to the floor of the cave. Tim followed her slowly, his mind reeling. South America? It seemed unlikely, though she had sounded so matter-of-fact. There was an airfield on Trull – he remembered his father telling him, now. If you wanted to leave the island in a hurry, that's what you would do: go to Trull by boat and catch a plane. But why should Mr Jones want to leave in a hurry, without telling anyone? And if he did want to, if he was in such a hurry, why had he wasted time taking them into the cave? It didn't make sense . . .

He reached the ground and saw Perdita, sitting beside Janey and singing with her. No one else was there.

'Where have they gone?' he whispered, half to himself, though he knew there was only one way they could go. Driven by a half-understood panic, he started along the tunnel. It twisted downhill and he realized, with a lift of his heart, that the men had not gone after all: he could see the yellow light of the lamp round a turn in the rocky stairway. They were talking. He was about to shout, when something in the tone of their voices warned him. He stayed quiet, crept towards the light, and listened.

'D'you think *I* like it?' Toffee Papers was saying. 'The boy'll be all right, and Smithie's girl – but the other one! Poor little thing!' His voice became thick with emotion and he blew his nose with a trumpeting sound. 'But let them go,' he went on, 'and they'll be back at the hotel before you can say knife, won't they? The balloon'll go up then. Tarbutt's only to phone and I won't get that plane. No, Campbell. They can stay here, I can phone from Trull, leave a message. Tarbutt'll get them out, they won't come to any harm. Bit hungry, bit cold, scared maybe – but no real harm.'

He seemed to be arguing to convince himself. It was rather the way he had talked on the beach. Suddenly Tim's heart began to thump. It was clear to him now. That story Toffee Papers had told! On and on about how clever the jewel thieves were! Was tying him up part of the cleverness? Was he one of the gang? Of course, that was it. He'd hidden his share of the loot up here on Skua and now, after three years, he had come to collect it. And OUT. And away . . .

Mr Campbell said something low, and Toffee Papers answered impatiently, 'Oh – all right. I'll leave my torch where they'll find it. As long as I have a chance to get clear. Once those kids begin to talk, there'll be dead trouble.' He laughed, and his laugh echoed coldly against the walls. 'For you, too, so you'd best not be too tender-hearted. You're in this, up to your neck . . .'

Campbell said slowly, 'We should warn Mr Smith . . .'

'And lose our own chance?' Toffee Papers' voice was indignant. 'What good would that do? Three of us locked up instead of one, that's all. Smithie can look after himself. He's good at that. I'm all right Jack – that's *his* motto. He's had it easy enough, these last years, sitting on his bottom up here, riding round in a Jaguar. And it's all his fault, when all's said and done – the whole thing was his idea from the beginning. Months he spent, getting to know me, talking me into it. . . . And then getting me to go stealing that kid's ruby. Risky to leave it, *he* said, it turned out to be risky for *me*, didn't it? Fat lot he cared . . .'

Tim could hold himself in no longer. He was in a wild fever of rage. He launched himself round the bend in the tunnel and straight at Toffee Papers. 'You beast, you horrible beast . . . you could have *killed* my Dad . . .' He catapulted straight into Toffee Papers' soft belly. Toffee Papers grunted and tried to catch hold of him, but he was a fat man, out of condition, and Tim got in several extremely satisfactory blows before Mr Campbell took him from behind, picked him up by the slack of his jacket and shook him as if he were a dirty puppy. Then he threw him on the ground, so hard that Tim felt as if the breath had been driven from his body.

The two men stood over him as he sprawled, half on one rocky step and half on another. Toffee Papers' eyes were streaming: one of Tim's wild punches had landed on his nose. His face was red with temper. 'You . . .' he began, let out a long, hissing breath and lifted his fist. Tim rolled in a ball to protect himself, but Campbell caught the other man's arm. 'No need for that,' he said quietly. 'Time's running short.'

He turned and clumped down the stairway, round a bend in the tunnel and out of sight. Once his hurricane lamp was gone, Toffee Papers' torch seemed to give very little light.

Tim said, 'You musn't leave us here. You *can't* . . .'

Toffee Papers smiled.

Tim tried to control the tremor in his voice. 'You told Mr Campbell you'd leave us the torch. You will, won't you?'

There was a little *click*. For a moment, coloured points of light swirled in front of Tim's eyes, then all was blackness, a cold, dead, empty blackness. He gave a little cry and Toffee Papers laughed. He switched on his torch again: behind its pale beam, Tim could see only the bones of his flat face and the pale shine of his eyes.

'D'you think I'd be such a fool?' Toffee Papers asked softly.

Tim thought: I can follow him, creep behind the light. Then when he's got in the boat, I can run and get help . . .

Toffee Papers said, 'No games, young man. No stalking games. I wouldn't want to hurt you. And *you* wouldn't want to scare your little sister, would you? She'd be scared if you left her.'

That was true, Tim realized. He couldn't leave Janey.

'So you just stay like a good boy,' Toffee Papers said in an encouraging, uncle-ish voice. 'Look after the girls until someone comes. Keep them cheerful. I wouldn't want to think either of them were scared or unhappy . . .'

He sighed, with what seemed genuine regret. In the torch beam, his eyes looked moist and sad, 'It's bad luck the way things have turned out. Really bad luck . . .'

Tim thought: I can't trust him. He changes too quickly – angry one minute, sorry the next. How could you trust a person like that? He had said he would telephone from Trull, but would he? And if he didn't . . .

It was no time to be brave. He said, softly and despairingly, 'Please don't leave us, Mr Jones. Not without a light. *Please* . . .

'Sorry, old chap,' Toffee Papers said. 'Really sorry . . .' And shaking his head sadly, he turned and followed Mr Campbell, round the next bend in the tunnel and out of sight . . .

Tim crawled back to the inner cavern on hands and knees, one hand on the wall of the tunnel. At least he had not come far, he could find his way back. But the brief journey taught him one thing: he could never, in this frightful darkness, find his way back through the maze of tunnels to the beach. There was nothing they could do. They would have to stay here, until help came.

If help came . . .

II

ABANDONED

'I DON'T mind staying here,' Janey said. 'It's nice, being in a cave, even if it is a bit cold. I like the noise my singing makes.'

And she began to sing, beating in time and occasionally stopping to listen to the echo.

Tim had told her that they had decided to stay here for a little, while the men explored the cave further. There was no point in frightening Janey. But he beckoned Perdita to the far end of the cavern and told her more of the truth: that Toffee Papers was in a hurry to get to Trull, and had deliberately abandoned them there.

'He *said* he was sorry,' he whispered, and then added, rather viciously, 'Crocodile tears.'

Perdita didn't know what a crocodile was. This seemed to interest her more than Mr Jones's eagerness to get to Trull. Tim tried to explain.

'Are there crocodiles in England, then?' she asked, when Tim had told her there were none on Skua, only in far-away, foreign places.

Tim sighed, and embarked on a geography lesson. Geography was not one of his best subjects, and, even if it had been, it would not have been easy to explain where Africa was to a girl who had never seen a map or a globe. Perdita was left with a rather confused impression that if she took the steamer to Oban and then turned right and walked for a while, she would eventually come to Africa which was full of sand and camels – sort of cows with humps, was how Tim described them – and naked black men and crocodiles. 'Why is it all sand? Why is it hot? Why doesn't it rain? Why are the men black?' she asked –

on and on until Tim grew tired and answered sullenly, 'Oh, *I* don't know . . .'

She looked surprised. 'Perhaps I'll find out more when I go to school. Though you don't seem to have learned much,' she added thoughtfully. Then she frowned. 'Why . . .'

'Oh *no*, not *again*,' Tim groaned.

'Just one more thing,' she pleaded. 'Why crocodile tears? Do crocodiles cry?'

'It's just a saying. It means he wasn't really sorry, just liked to think he was. I mean . . .' – he tried to think it out – 'I suppose it means that crocodiles often have water in their eyes because they live in rivers, but they eat you up, just the same.' For a second, he was rather pleased with this explanation, but then the import of it struck him with a shock of horror. It could mean, in this case, that Toffee Papers might feel sorry enough to say he would send someone to find them, but he might not be sorry enough to *do* it. 'If he doesn't tell anyone we're here,' he began, and stopped. Perdita was older than Janey, but there was no point in frightening her either. Unless . . .

'Are you really a witch?' he asked suddenly.

'I can see through walls and round corners . . .' Perdita began happily, but Tim stopped her.

'Oh, I know all that. But can you see in the *dark*. Could you get us out of here?'

Perdita was silent.

'*Try*,' Tim urged her. 'Shut your eyes and *try* . . .'

Perdita shut her eyes. 'What do you want me to see?'

'Just . . . just if you can see the way out.'

She stood still, her eyes obediently closed. Her face was expressionless and secret, and, watching her, Tim felt a sudden lifting of his heart. Suppose there were witches, after all? He didn't believe in them, at least, he hadn't believed in them, but now he wanted to, very much. Perhaps that was a part of magic: if you believed in a thing, it would help it to come true. Determinedly, he shut his own eyes and stood, tense and rigid, while his lips moved silently. 'I believe in witches, I believe in witches, I believe in witches . . .'

'What *are* you doing?' Perdita asked in an amazed voice. He opened his eyes and saw she was staring at him.

'Nothing,' he said self-consciously. Then, *'Was it any good?'*

She shook her head. 'I tried to think about the way we came in. But I can't. I couldn't find my way out in the dark. Not in the pitch black.' She shivered suddenly. 'What if no one comes with a light?' she said, her eyes wide and startled.

'Don't be frightened,' Tim said gently. She looked so little and thin, as young as Janey . . .

'I'm not . . .' Perdita stopped. She had a new feeling, one she could not remember having before, a sort of icy shudder, running down her chest and into her stomach as if she had just swallowed something very cold. 'Am I frightened?' she whispered, and all Tim's pity vanished, and he had a brutal desire to shake her.

'If you're not, you ought to be,' he said. 'If he doesn't tell anyone where we are, or tells them too late . . .' *Of course he wouldn't telephone from Trull*, he suddenly realized. It wouldn't be safe for *him*. He would wait until he got to Glasgow or London or some airport where he could get a direct connexion to South America. He might wait even longer: Tim had a horrifying vision of Toffee Papers' tender conscience acting in a week's time, on the other side of the world. 'Then we'll die,' he said bleakly. 'We'll be dead of cold and starvation . . .'

Perdita's lip began to tremble. He said quickly, 'What kind of magic *can* you do? I don't mean seeing round corners or thinking you're flying . . .'

Perdita said slowly, 'I can make Annie do things sometimes. If I stare and stare. Or, if I'm in bed, I can make her come upstairs and say good night to me.'

That wasn't magic, Tim thought resignedly. Sometimes,

when his mother and father had been angry, and sent him to
bed in disgrace, he had done that sort of thing himself: concentrated hard and willed them to come up to him. It usually
worked, but only, he recognized regretfully, because they
were sorry they had been mean to him. Still, it was a chance.
Their only chance.

'Could you make Annie come here?' he said.

Perdita laughed. It was an odd sound in that murky cave.
'Oh she couldn't,' she said. 'She's too rheumaticky. She gets
it in her knees terribly badly, this time of year.'

Tim thought this a curiously practical argument for a
witch. But perhaps she knew her own business best. 'Well,'
he said slowly, 'someone else, then. Anyone would do, though
perhaps it would work best if it was someone you knew well.
I mean, you can fix your mind on them better.'

'I don't know anyone else, except Mr Smith,' Perdita said.

Mr Smith. Mr Smith was a crook. The leader of the gang.
This much Tim had gathered when he was listening to Toffee
Papers, but he had not paid the discovery much attention until
now: he had been far too worried about their immediate
plight. Now, he thought a minute. All that talk of Mr Jones's
about hiding the loot in a safe place – well, Skua was a safe
place, wasn't it? As safe as you were likely to get. There was no
policeman. No one came, or hardly ever. If you just sat still and
minded your own business . . .

'When did Mr Smith come to Skua?' he asked.

Perdita thought. 'Not last summer, not the summer before,
but the summer before that. The summer I was eight.'

'Three years.' Tim whistled softly. 'He *must* be the leader of
the gang!'

'What is a gang?' Perdita asked and Tim tried to explain to
her about gangs and jewel thieves and organized robberies. It
was as difficult as explaining about Africa. Tim realized that
although she had listened to him, when he read out the newspaper story on the beach, she had not really understood what it

was about. There were no criminals on Skua and Perdita had never seen television or read a book. Understanding this, he tried to make his explanation as simple as possible, but her expression remained perplexed.

'But Mr Smith's not a bad man,' she said finally. 'He's been good to me and Annie.'

Tim drew a deep breath and began to say that perhaps even a bad man could be good in parts, when Janey called to him.

'Tim, Tim . . . where are you? I'm bored with singing.'

'Coming,' he shouted across the cave, and then whispered to Perdita, 'Make Mr Smith come to find us then. Try *hard*.'

He went over to Janey who was looking sulky. 'You've been away ages,' she complained. 'And I'm getting cold and I'm getting hungry.'

'We weren't far. Just the other side of the cave.'

'Looking for rubies? Did you find one?' Janey asked eagerly.

'No. I don't think there are any.'

Although he had determined not to worry or frighten Janey, he could not quite keep the misery out of his voice. She felt for his hand and squeezed it encouragingly. 'Never mind, Tim. When the police catch our burglar, you'll get your own ruby back, won't you?'

Precious little chance of catching Toffee Papers, Tim thought glumly. By the time they got out – *if* they got out – Toffee Papers would be miles away on the other side of the world. And the jewels, too – or rather, his share of them. Tim sighed. If only they could escape before Mr Smith disappeared, too! He sighed again, longingly: newspaper headlines flashed in front of his eyes. BOY CAPTURES JEWEL THIEF. MYSTERY OF MISSING JEWELS SOLVED – BY TIM HOGGART. QUEEN REWARDS GALLANT BOY DETECTIVE. SUPERINTENDENT SAYS: THIS IS THE KIND OF BOY WE WANT IN THE POLICE FORCE.

Perhaps that last headline was a bit long. It could be put under one of the others, in smaller print. Tim sat, his eyes half-closed, dreaming.

'I tried,' Perdita said beside him. 'But I don't think it will work.' She paused. 'Mr Smith said, if I played with other children I'd lose my Powers,' she said. Then her face crumpled. 'I don't want to stay here, Tim . . .'

Tim glanced apprehensively at Janey, but she said composedly, 'If Perdita wants to go now, I don't mind. I'm getting a little bit cold. Shall we go, Tim?' And she stood up waiting. Waiting for Tim to take her hand and lead her out of the cave and home.

Tim looked at her helplessly and the full horror of their predicament really dawned on him for the first time. 'We'll die,' he had said to Perdita, but he hadn't really believed it then: it had just seemed like a story he was telling himself. Now, looking at Janey, he knew it wasn't a story.

'Oh – don't let's go yet. It's such fun here.' He heard his own voice as if it belonged to someone else. A scared someone else.

'What's the matter? You sound funny.' Janey put her head on one side and frowned, the way she did when she was trying to hear what people meant, rather than just what they said.

Tim swallowed hard. He musn't tell her the truth, not yet. The best thing would be to keep her happy, playing with her and singing, until she got tired and went to sleep. There was no point in frightening her unnecessarily. Someone might come to find them after all. And, even if they did not, there was still no point in Janey knowing how really terrible their situation was. Even if she came to understand in the end, it might be easier for her when she was weak and apathetic with exhaustion and hunger. That would be like being ill, perhaps. When he had had measles, last year, he had felt so weak afterwards that he would not have minded much if someone had told him he was going to die. As long as he stayed with her and held her close, it might not be so dreadful for her. As long as he stayed alive long enough, so she could die in his arms . . .

There was a horrible great lump in his throat. He forced his voice over it. 'Let's sing something, shall we? All together? What about *Row, row, row down the river . . .*'

Janey touched his hand. 'Have you got a stomach ache?'

'He's frightened,' Perdita said. 'I'm frightened, too. It's a horrible feeling, like feeling sick. I never had it before.'

Tim said quickly, 'It's because she's stopped being a witch and become like an ordinary person. Witches are never frightened and they don't have shadows and their hands are always cold. Hers aren't cold now.'

'They never were,' Janey said. She was not to be diverted. 'Why is she frightened, Tim? Why are you frightened?'

Tim pulled a warning face at Perdita, but he was too late: she had already begun to speak. 'Because we can't get out of the cave,' she said. 'Mr Jones brought us in here and left us here and he's gone away with the light. And Mr Campbell too. Tim says it's because Mr Jones is a jewel thief and a bad man and . . .'

'Toffee Papers!' Janey said in a loud, excited voice. '*Was* he the burglar, Tim? Did he steal your ruby?'

Tim told her what he had learned, spinning out the tale as long as possible, hoping that she had not really understood the full meaning of what Perdita had said, or, if she had, that she would forget it in the excitement of hearing the mystery solved.

'He ought to be put in prison,' she said when he had finished. 'Knocking our Dad down. And if that Mr Smith is a robber too, *he* ought to be put in prison. We'll tell Mr Tarbutt and he'll see to it, won't he? Let's go back and tell him now.'

Tim could not speak. When he didn't move to take her hand she bent, groping for him, and tugged at the sleeve of his jacket. 'Come on. Oh – you are *lazy*,' she scolded.

'We can't . . .' Tim looked despairingly at Perdita.

'We can't get out of the cave,' she cried. 'Oh Janey, don't you understand?'

She stood between them, looking puzzled. 'Why can't we?' she asked. 'Why can't we just go back the way we came? Toffee Papers did, didn't he?'

'He had a torch,' Tim said. 'He could see. We can't, it's dark . . .' It seemed impossible to explain this to Janey. 'We can't find our way back in the dark,' he mumbled.

For a moment, Janey said nothing. She seemed to be puzzling something out. Then she said, slowly, 'I think *I* could, though. I don't mind the dark.'

12

A KIND OF MAGIC

SOMETIMES Tim tried to imagine what the world must seem like to Janey. He would close his eyes and walk about, listening and feeling. But it was impossible for him to know what darkness was really like for her, as impossible as knowing, even though you could swim under water, what water must be like for a fish. Or air for a bird.

Or dark, for Janey. Looking at her, he caught his breath. When someone said 'I can't see in the dark,' it must seem very strange to her, as strange as it would to a fish – if you could talk to a fish – if you said 'I can't breathe under water.'

'Are you sure you can find the way back?' he asked slowly. She only needed to be shown round a strange house once, but if she got lost there were always people to help her. Once in the tunnel there would be no one. He and Perdita would be helpless. Blind.

Perdita said, 'But *how* can she find her way?'

'Just the same way I always do,' Janey said. She was silent for a minute, as if wondering how to explain what that way was. Could *he* explain, Tim thought, how he could see with his eyes? Janey smiled suddenly. 'It's like Perdita's second sight, I suppose.'

They led her to the mouth of the tunnel. Once there, she put her hand on the wall. Tim put his hand on her shoulder and Perdita clutched the back of his wind-cheater. They began to walk down the rocky stairs. For the first few yards, while the light lasted, Janey's pace seemed slow to them; then as soon as the last blue glimmer vanished and they were in the dark, it seemed terrifyingly fast. They stumbled, panic-stricken.

'Go slower, Janey,' Tim begged.

'I'm going slow,' she said indignantly. 'Why don't you walk properly, 'stead of banging about all over the place?'

'I don't know how,' Tim said humbly. It was true. Walking in the pitch dark was different – and frightening: you lifted your foot and it was like stepping off a cliff into black, empty air.

Janey stood still. 'Feel,' she said, after a pause. 'Feel with your feet. That's what I do.'

She moved on again. The two behind her began to learn. Keeping one hand on the wall, they slid their feet forwards, feeling with their toes and the balls of their feet. Their progress became steadier and their panic ebbed a little.

'That's better,' Janey said. 'You're doing fine – just fine.'

She spoke in the bright, encouraging voice her mother sometimes used to her, when she was trying to do something that was hard for a blind girl to do.

Once she stopped. 'I'm listening,' she explained, and Tim and Perdita tried to listen too, but though they strained their ears, they heard nothing. It was horrible standing still and waiting in that cold, silent blackness. Tim remembered the ravine they had passed over. That terrible drop! Janey had not seen it, she couldn't know how dangerous it was.

He whispered hoarsely, 'Janey – there's a sort of hole in the rock, with water a long way down.'

'I know,' she said, quite calmly. 'Wait a minute.' She stamped with her feet. 'It's soon – can't you hear? The ground's sort of hollow.'

She was right. They couldn't hear – or feel – the hollowness, but a few steps later they heard the water. Miles below them, miles and miles. ... Tim stood still suddenly, and Perdita bumped into him.

'Come on,' Janey said. 'It's all right close to the wall.'

She led on and they followed, fearful but trusting her. They had to trust her. They went on, slowly shuffling, and the water sounded loud on their left. They were crossing the ravine. Tim tried so hard to see into the darkness that his eyeballs burned.

'Past it now,' Janey said.

On a little farther. 'Tim,' Perdita said. 'Tim . . .'

'Yes?'

'Tim . . .' she repeated slowly, and then the words tumbled out in a rush. 'You know what you said about Mr Smith. Well, if you tell Mr Tarbutt, will he go to prison?'

'I expect so.'

She let out a long sigh.

Tim felt uncomfortable. 'If he's a thief, he ought to go to prison. We'll have to tell Mr Tarbutt what we know, and I expect we'll have to tell the police, too.' This prospect was rather exciting. Surely Perdita would find it exciting, too? 'Perhaps they'll want to talk to you as well. Perhaps you'll have to give evidence.' She made no response and he went on, encouragingly, 'You might even have to be a witness in court. Tell them how Mr Smith wouldn't let you go to school or mix with other children. That shows he had something to hide, you see, so it will be important evidence. You might even get your picture in the papers . . .'

'Oh, do shut up,' Janey wailed. 'How can I see if you talk?'

One more tentative step, then another. Was it his imagination, or was Janey's progress less certain now? She seemed to be stopping more often. She had stopped now, and they all stood still, rigid, waiting . . .

Fear grew in Tim's mind. He should never have let Janey attempt this . . . this madness. Of course she thought she could do it, but she was only nine, she had no real idea of danger. Less idea, perhaps, than most children: although she had always been encouraged to be independent and do things for herself, there had always been someone close at hand to see no harm came to her . . .

Perdita said, 'Go on, Janey.' Her voice was impatient, not frightened. That was because she believed in magic, Tim thought. He knew – had a glimmering, anyway – of how Janey could find her way. Perdita had none: it was a kind of magic to her.

Suddenly Janey shouted. 'Aaaaaaah . . .'

Tim almost screamed with fright. Hysteria rose up in him. He tried to suppress it and speak in an ordinary voice. 'What on earth did you do that for?'

'This is one of the places where we shouted,' Janey said. 'I think I can tell where we are, by the echo.'

They began to shout. Their cries rang back at them from the unseen walls. Then they stood silent and listened to the echoes die away.

'Once more,' Janey said. They shouted again. And listened. Janey gave a little sigh. She left the wall and walked slowly, her hands spread out. She bumped into rock, sooner than she expected, perhaps, because she gave a little cry. Then her shoulder moved under Tim's hand as she began to feel the surface of the rock, stroking and patting and muttering under her breath: *'There was a little crack, my fingers went in it, only it was the other hand because I was going the other way, and there was a bit jutting out lower down, I banged my knee on it and it bleeded a little and stuck up my sock so it must have been a bit sharp . . .'*

Tim held his breath. Then Janey gave a low, triumphant giggle. 'I'm *right*,' she said. 'This is the right place. In a minute, we'll be able to hear the sea.'

And they did. But before they heard the sea, they saw the light, at first just a faint paling of the darkness ahead and then the darkness seemed to form round to make a shape, an arch. It was the mouth of the tunnel that led into the main cave and out to the beach and the sea . . .

Janey seemed to be moving very slowly now. 'Hurry,' Tim urged, pushing her from behind, and then letting her go and running past her, towards the light.

Perdita followed him. They reached the main cave, tumbling over each other like puppies. The light was grey because the day was darkening, not only with evening but also with a curtain of rain, blowing into the cave and hissing on the shingle, but it was *light*. Light – after that terrible blackness. Perdita and Tim shouted with joy. They shouted so loud that for a little Janey could not make herself heard.

'Tim . . . Tim . . .'

He heard her at last. She had come out of the tunnel and was standing in the cave, her hands out in front of her. 'I can't see any more, there aren't any more walls,' she said.

The other two fell silent. They looked at each other and then down at their feet. Neither of them spoke.

'What's the matter?' Janey asked. She smiled broadly and wrapped her arms across her chest, hugging herself with delight. 'I found the way out, didn't I? You'd never have found it yourselves . . .'

Tim ran to her, put his arms round her and hugged and kissed her. 'You were wonderful,' he said. 'A heroine, Janey. You saved our lives.'

'Oh, it wasn't very hard,' Janey said modestly. 'Can we go home now? I'm so hungry.'

They went to the mouth of the cave. The sharp rain prickled their faces and hands and the blustering wind caught their breath and almost blew them back inside. Tim had to put his arms round Janey, to steady her.

'Let's wait a bit. It'll be awful, going back along the cliff in this,' he said. 'Absolutely awful.'

But Janey pouted. 'I don't mind the rain. I'm hungry.' He looked at her and saw she looked pale and tired, suddenly, as if the effort of getting them out of the cave had exhausted her. 'I want to go home,' she said, and the pout turned into a miserable little trembling of her lips. 'I want my Mum.'

His heart smote him. 'All right,' he said gently. 'Don't cry, Janey. We'll be home quite soon.'

He put his arm round her, to protect her as much as he could from the wind, and began to help her over the rocks towards the cliff path. 'Come on, Perdita,' he shouted over his shoulder, but she answered something he couldn't catch and turned towards the cliff where the water of the lower fall crashed on to the beach like thunder. 'Come back, idiot,' Tim shouted, but either she didn't hear, or had determined to take no notice: she began to climb up the side of the fall.

Tim hesitated, torn. That was a dangerous climb, even for a girl who was used to cliffs and mountains. But he daren't go after her, he daren't leave Janey . . .

'Where's Perdita?' she asked now. 'I want Perdita . . .'

Tim remembered what Perdita had said yesterday, when he told her about his climb down to the cave. 'She's gone up the cliff,' he said, 'that's the quickest way home for her.'

'I expect she's hurrying home to tell about horrible old Toffee Papers leaving us in the cave,' Janey said. There was an ominous shake in her voice as if she had just realized that this was a frightening thing to have happened. 'Just like the Babes in the Wood,' she said. 'D'you remember, Tim? The wicked man took them into the wood and left them and they died and the robins came and covered them with leaves.'

'It's all right, we aren't dead, are we?' Tim soothed her. They were off the rocks now, and on the path between the high walls of the cliff. It was more sheltered here, though overhead the wind cracked like a giant whip. 'But if she tells Mr Smith . . .' Tim began, and stopped. If she told Mr Smith, told him everything, he would know the police were likely to be after him and he would try to escape, like Toffee Papers. 'We better hurry . . .' Tim said.

He set too fast a pace for Janey. Though she tried to keep up, she was very tired and began to sob under her breath and stumble. He slowed to match her pace, though it was an effort: his own tiredness had vanished at the marvellous prospect of bringing a criminal to justice. Why, he would be the hero of the hour! And what would his father say? His father, who had always refused to believe anything really exciting could ever happen. *Too much imagination, old chap?* He would never dare say that again, Tim thought, and laughed aloud.

When they came to the end of the sheltered stretch, the path along the cliff face was as slippery as he had feared it would be. He was too occupied, then, encouraging and comforting Janey, to dream of future glory, too occupied, even, to be frightened, although the storm had whipped the sea below them into a witch's cauldron of black waves and flying spray. By the time they reached the bay, Janey was crying properly and could walk no further. With an immense effort, Tim heaved her up into his arms and carried her a few yards before he collapsed on the beach. 'I can't,' he gasped, 'you weigh about a *ton*.'

She clung to him, crying, and they huddled together, too cold and wet now to think of anything except the little shelter they could give each other from the rain and the wind that flung stinging sand into their faces. The wind howled and screamed round them as if it were trying to tear the clothes from their backs: it made such a noise that they could hear nothing else. They did not hear Mr Tarbutt until he stood above them and jerked them to their feet.

He was wearing black oilskins. His tow-coloured hair lay in strands over his face.

'Silly young fool,' he said angrily to Tim. 'I'd have thought you had more sense . . .'

He picked Janey up in his arms, and for once she did not protest. He carried her over to the shelter of the great rock and set her down there for a minute, while he wiped the sand from her face.

'We found Mr Jones,' she said, when her sobs had quietened. 'How'd you find us?'

He explained that he had been searching since five o'clock. It was now almost nine. He had been to the bay before, but seen no sign of them. 'You've led me a fine dance, all over the island,' he scolded. 'It was just chance I came here a second time . . .' Then his eyes narrowed, as if the other thing Janey had said had only now come home to him. '*What*'s this about Mr Jones?'

'He stole Tim's ruby,' Janey said shrilly. 'He was the burglar. And he took us into the cave and left us there, he's not a nice man at all, he's a horrible *beast*...'

He eyed her incredulously. 'But what ...?' he began, and then decided not to question her further. 'Best get home,' he muttered. 'It'll wait ...'

But Tim was not content to wait. He ran beside Mr Tarbutt and Janey, shouting to tell the man all he had heard and all he had guessed. Mr Tarbutt did his best to listen, although the climb up from the bay and round the boggy slopes of Ben Luin was a hard one, in the rain and the wind. From time to time he nodded, and the rain flew out of the brim of his black oilskin hat. He had unbuttoned his coat and tucked Janey inside it: all Tim could see of her was her long wet hair, streaming over Mr Tarbutt's shoulder.

'So we'll have to telephone the police,' Tim gasped out finally. 'Just as soon as we get back.'

They were over the top of the ridge and going down towards Skuaphort. Mr Tarbutt stopped in the lee of the ruined cottage to rest a minute and adjust Janey's weight. Incredibly, she seemed to have gone to sleep, breathing with little snores, her thumb half in, half out of, her mouth. Mr Tarbutt grinned at Tim over her head. 'I reckon they may be here already, lad,' he said. 'Your mother, too, poor soul. Worried out of her mind about you.'

As Tim said, Mrs Hoggart had a good memory for faces. She had remembered, a little after she had spoken to Mr Tarbutt, exactly where she had seen Mr Jones – or, rather, his photograph – before. She had told the police in Oban. 'Some time ago and something to do with a robbery,' was all she could tell them, but it had been enough. The police not only knew about Mr Jones: they knew he was on Skua.

'They'd kept an eye on him these last three years apparently,' Mr Tarbutt said, when he had explained that Mrs Hoggart had telephoned again, from the police station in Oban, just as he had returned from his first, fruitless expedition to the bay. 'So when he came north, it was a matter of routine to inform the local police. Not that there was anything *against* him, you understand . . .' Mr Tarbutt hesitated. 'Not until he attacked your father, that is. It seems he'd done nothing suspicious since the jewels were stolen – nothing to show he wasn't as innocent as he claimed to be. Just got on with his job, and then, after three years, a little holiday on Skua . . .'

Tim was almost too breathless with excitement to speak. 'What about Mr Smith?' he managed to gasp, but Mr Tarbutt shrugged his shoulders and gave Tim a doubtful, sideways look.

'Nothing on him, far as I know. Just a quiet gentleman who minds his own business. Still, if you tell the police what you've told me, I daresay they'll pay him a little visit.'

'He'll have gone by then,' Tim said glumly. The wind was gentler now they were down off the ridge and when they reached the stone road, he was able to trot beside Mr Tarbutt quite comfortably, telling him about Perdita and how she had gone home up the cliff. 'She'll have warned him,' he said. 'She knows he's a thief and he ought to go to prison, I told her, but she didn't like it much. She said he'd been good to her and Annie.'

'Poor little lass,' Mr Tarbutt said.

'It would have been poor all of us,' Tim said indignantly. 'If that horrible Mr Jones had had his way.'

Mr Tarbutt made no direct reply to this, but he shifted Janey's weight against his shoulder and took Tim's hand. He held it tight and comfortingly, until they reached the little town and saw the lights of the police launch, rocking in the bay, and Mrs Hoggart waiting, wild-eyed and frantic in the doorway of the hotel. After she had hugged and kissed them and heard their story – which led to more hugging and kissing and a few, grateful tears – she told them that Mr Jones had never got to Trull. Will Campbell's boat had been near foundering in the rough sea when the daily ferry, that ran between Trull and the mainland, had picked them up and taken them to Oban.

Mr Jones had been arrested as he walked off the boat.

13

A LITTLE WILD THING, HALF-CRAZED

THE witch's daughter came down to the loch. The hills
sheltered it from the wind, but the heavy rain steamed on to it,
making the mist rise, white and thick. It swirled round her,
clinging in damp pearls to her rain-soaked hair. She had run so
fast that the cold breath sobbed in her throat and sent spikes of
pain down into her chest: as she stumbled on to the pebbly
shore of the loch, the greedy black water sucked at her boots
and she stumbled and almost fell.

Recovering, she stood still a minute. The Lake Horse had
come out of the loch on a night like this, and taken her mother.
Annie MacLaren had said so, and Perdita believed it, as she
believed the other things the old woman had told her. Indeed,
Perdita was sure she had often seen the Lake Horse, racing
across the surface of the water. He had never frightened her.
Why should he? All he could do, would be to take her to live
with her mother under the surface of the loch.

But tonight, peering into the mist, she *was* afraid. Too
frightened to move suddenly, too frightened, even, to whimper. Fear – this kind of cold, rigid fear – was new to her.
Witches are never frightened. Perhaps what Tim had said in
the cave was true: she had stopped being a witch, and become
ordinary, like other children.

She thought: but ordinary children can't breathe under
water. If the Lake Horse came for her tonight, she would
drown. She began to stumble round the shore of the loch, no
longer a witch, just a frightened little girl. And when she saw
him, out of the corner of her eye – huge, white, with a great,
flowing mane – she began to scream loudly and piercingly, like
any other frightened child.

As she screamed, the Lake Horse began to change shape. His neck extended, became thin and tenuous, until it drifted away from his body, and his body itself began to dissolve, to melt . . .

Perdita stopped screaming. 'You're nothing . . . just *mist*,' she said in a loud, contemptuous voice, and ran away from the loch, up the side of the bank towards Luinpool.

Annie MacLaren was standing by the back door, an oil lamp in her hand. 'Where've you been, lady? He's been on at me, worrying.'

Perdita ran past her, through the kitchen and into the hall. Her footsteps slowed as she reached the door of Mr Smith's room, and she stood outside it for a moment, her heart thumping. Mr Jones was a bad man and he had left them in the cave – to die, Tim had said. He had said Mr Smith was a bad man, too. If that was true, what would *he* do, when she admitted what she had done? Then she remembered that he had often been kind to her, drew a long, shaky breath, and opened the door.

He was lying back in his chair, an open book face downwards on his lap. He looked up and asked what she wanted in an irritated voice that would ordinarily have sent her scuttling from the room: she wasn't frightened of Mr Smith, but Annie had taught her to respect his moods.

He seemed surprised when she stood her ground. 'Anything the matter?' he asked, quite kindly, sitting up in his chair and closing his book.

She swallowed hard: 'They're going to tell the police about you,' she said.

Mr Smith picked up the poker and thumped thoughtfully at a lump of peat on the fire, making the sparks fly. Then he looked up at her, smiling. 'Who's they?'

'The boy and girl from the hotel. Tim says you'll go to prison.'

'Prison?' Mr Smith said. He still smiled, but his fist was clenched on the handle of the poker. 'Does he say what for?'

Perdita looked down at her feet. 'He says you're a bad man.'
'What kind of bad man?' he asked mildly.

Encouraged by his gentleness, she looked at him. 'A thief. He says you're the head of a gang of jewel thieves.'

Mr Smith laughed, rather too loudly. 'That's a good story. I gather you've been talking, witch. Haven't you?' She did not answer and, after a minute he said slowly, 'I see. . . . So you told them all about me, eh? What did you tell them, exactly?'

'Nothing. Not about you.' Her lips felt dry and she moistened them with the tip of her tongue. 'I just showed Janey my lucky stone and they found out Mr Jones gave it to me that night he came here. And when he ran away and left us in Carlin's Cave . . .'

'When he did *what*?'

Stumblingly, frightened by his look and the sudden harshness in his voice, Perdita explained about the cave and how Mr Jones had taken them in and left them there, without a light. 'Tim said he left us there to die, just so he could get away,' she said, and her lip quivered.

Mr Smith stared into the fire. 'The fool – oh the *fool*,' he said. 'My God – if they believe that, they'll take the island apart.' He was silent, then, for what seemed to Perdita a terribly long time and when he began to speak again it was very softly, as if he were talking to himself. 'Who'll believe it, though? A child's story? *If* he's got clean away . . .' Suddenly he dropped the poker on to the hearth with a clatter and said, 'I've got to know . . .'

He looked at Perdita. 'Come here, little witch,' he said. His voice was gentle again, but it was a forced gentleness. She went to him reluctantly and he held her fast by the wrist as Mr Jones had done, the night he came. 'Look at me.' She looked at him and saw her own reflection in the dark pools of his glasses. 'Listen,' Mr Smith said, 'there's something you've got to do for me . . .'

A little later the white Jaguar drove down to Skuaphort. Just outside the town it stopped and pulled off the road into a farm gateway. Perdita got out. The wind was very strong now and seemed to blow her like a leaf, down the stony road towards the town and the hotel.

At the closed door, she hesitated. *Find Tim*, Mr Smith had said, *find Tim and ask him....* Though the hotel door was closed, it would not be locked, she knew: no one locked doors on Skua. She could steal in and up to his room. She knew which it was – first on the left at the top of the stairs, Janey had told her. She put her hand in the door, and then withdrew it, her courage failing. The bar was dark, but light streamed from the lounge window into an empty sun parlour that had been built against the side of the hotel. The parlour had a door that gave on to the street. As soon as she turned the handle, the wind blew the door inwards: once inside, it took all her strength to close it. She climbed on a crate of empty beer bottles and peered through the window into the lounge.

Tim was there. He was sitting by the fire in his dressing-gown between his mother and a large man Perdita had never seen on the island before. He had close-cropped, gingery hair and a large, amiable, pale face. He was talking. She could see his lips move but the window was closed and she could not hear what he said.

The policeman had a soft, Scotch voice. He rolled his R's beautifully. He had a brown mole low down on one pale cheek, and while he talked it waggled up and down.

'So you see,' he was saying, 'we'd kept tabs on Pr-r-att. Or Jones, if you like, since that's the name you've got used to. We didn't believe his story, but since he sat tight and did nothing, there was nothing we could do, either. Not directly. Inquiries were made, of course. There was this gang he'd talked of – well, you know most of the time the police have a pretty good **idea** what most of the criminal population is up to, and this wasn't any gang they could put a finger on. More likely there was just one other man – possibly two, but probably one. Someone who'd got at Jones – someone pretty persuasive, because firms in the jewel trade are careful whom they employ, you know, and there was no suggestion he'd been up to anything of this sort before. Well – who had he been seeing? No one, it seemed, except a few innocent neighbours, until we came up with *this* man. It turned out that he'd been seen with a stranger several times, walking in the park, talking in a local pub. That was some time before the robbery took place – no one remembered seeing him afterwards. Naturally we asked Jones, but he denied it. At least, he didn't exactly deny it, he just said he was a friendly sort and often talked to strangers, but that he didn't remember talking to anyone in particular during the last six months. . . . Well, we couldn't press it. You can't hound a man without evidence and there wasn't any evidence. Only suspicion. He *did* seem to have a bit more money than he'd had before. He launched out a bit – new washing machine, new motor mower, that sort of thing. Not enough to act on, just enough to make us wonder . . .'

'Sit on the loot,' Tim said. 'Don't spend it. Or only carefully, bit by bit. That's what he said.'

The policeman nodded. 'That's what it looked like. That's what our people in London thought, anyway.'

'Did you have a description of the stranger?' Tim asked eagerly.

This was, he thought, the most exciting night of his life. For a while after they got back, Janey had been the centre of attention as she deserved to be. Now, hugged and kissed and sated with admiration, she had been put to bed with a sedative, and it was Tim's turn. Here he was, at nearly eleven o'clock, sitting with a real live plainclothes policeman who had listened gravely and courteously to all he had to say and was now telling him a marvellous story that might have come out of a newspaper or a book.

'Description?' the policeman said. 'Not one that helps much. Medium height, medium weight, medium colouring . . .'

'It *could* be Mr Smith, though?'

'Or a great many other people.' The policeman smiled at Tim. 'Listen, young man. I've been very interested in what you've told me, don't think I haven't, but I'm afraid I'll have to warn you, too. Don't go spreading stories about Mr Smith. There's such a thing as slander. Nor about Mr Jones, either. We're interested to know what he's been up to, on Skua, and it seems from what you've told me that he *has* been up to something. But only *seems*, mind you. We've no real proof he was up to anything at all . . .'

'He came to collect his share of the loot,' Tim said positively. 'And he was going to fly off with it to South America.'

'It's possible. But we've no proof of it. On the face of it, he and Mr Campbell were on an innocent fishing trip when they got into difficulties. And when we picked him up, he'd got nothing on him.' He grinned suddenly. 'Just a bag of toffees! We're holding him, of course, but we can't do that for long.'

'What d'you mean?' Mrs Hoggart's voice was indignant. 'He assaulted my husband.'

'He admits he pushed him,' the policeman said slowly. 'He says he went into the wrong room by mistake and when your husband came in he was startled. He pushed past Mr Hoggart to get out of the room and then, when the accident happened, he simply lost his nerve and kept quiet about it.' The policeman paused. 'The way he tells it, it sounds like a – well, a regrettable *accident*.'

'But the children!' Mrs Hoggart cried. 'He took those poor children into the cave and left them there. That was a terrible thing, a wicked thing . . .'

The policeman sighed. 'Well – I got on the phone to Oban while you were putting the little lass to bed. They had a word with him and rang me back. He says he met the children on the beach and played with them a bit. They did go into the cave, he says, and he was a bit worried about leaving them there, but he and Campbell were going fishing and he supposed they'd be safe enough. He assumed they had torches, he said, and though he wouldn't have let *his* children wander about alone, if *their* parents weren't worried, it wasn't his business. Thoughtless, a bit casual, but not *criminal*, you see . . .'

Tim could hardly believe his ears. He said shrilly, 'But you don't believe him, do you?'

The policeman looked at him thoughtfully. 'What I believe isn't evidence, you know. And I'm afraid that when we find Campbell – he just walked off the ferry, we'd no reason for holding him since we'd not heard this story then – he'll back up Mr Jones's story. Jones seemed confident he would.'

'Mr Campbell didn't want to leave us in the cave,' Tim said. He felt depressed and helpless. He knew what he had said was true, he had *heard* Toffee Papers talking in the cave, but apparently no one would believe him. It wasn't *fair*, he thought childishly. Feeling miserable and sullen, he slouched back in his chair, scowling, and then became aware that the policeman was looking at him in an interested way.

'Didn't he?' the policeman said. 'That's a useful thing to know . . .' He looked straight in front of him and appeared to address the air. 'If we get hold of him before he hears the children are safe, if we tell him they're still missing . . . there's just a chance we may get at the truth . . .'

Tim gasped and sat bolt upright. 'You *do* believe me then?' he said. Excitement buzzed in his head.

The policeman half-smiled.

'Of course he does, Tim,' Mrs Hoggart said, smiling too. 'Do you think he's been wasting his time, talking to you?'

'It wouldn't hold up in court, though,' the policeman said regretfully. He looked at Mrs Hoggart. 'Your son is an imaginative boy, isn't he? I happen to believe he is also a truthful one, but it is a very highly coloured story – just the sort of story an imaginative boy might dream up. Thieves, diamonds, being abandoned in caves, stolen rubies . . .'

'Janey knows the ruby was stolen,' Tim said. 'She's certain – it was she told *me*.'

The policeman was silent. It was Mrs Hoggart who said, very gently, 'Tim darling, you and I know Janey. But no one else will believe that.'

'*Perdita*, then,' Tim burst out. 'She knows, too. Not about my ruby, I mean, and she didn't know what Mr Jones said in the cave, only what I told her, but she knows he's a friend of Mr Smith's. She saw him there one night and he had a box of jewels and he gave her one . . .'

'So you said. But this girl . . .' The policeman hesitated. 'From what I hear she would not exactly be a reliable witness. Can't read, can't write, Mr Tarbutt says, a little wild thing, half-crazed . . .'

'She's *not*,' Tim said stubbornly. 'I mean she doesn't know where Africa is, and she didn't know what a diamond was, and she says her mother was a witch. But she's quite . . .'

'Sensible,' was what he had been going to say, but he saw the broad, involuntary grin on the policeman's face and stopped.

'I wouldn't care to put her in the witness box,' the policeman said. 'But I'll certainly have a word with her. With Mr Smith too, and maybe . . .'

He stopped mid-sentence and was out of his chair and at the french windows that led into the sun parlour almost before Tim and his mother had taken in what had alerted him: a splintering crash outside the dark windows of the lounge and a sudden, frightened cry . . .

The policeman moved with surprising speed for such a bulky man. By the time Tim and his mother had reached the sun parlour, he had scooped Perdita up out of the tumbled wreckage of beer crates and deck chairs, and was holding her by the arm. 'Perdita,' Tim cried, but her eyes were terrified, unrecognizing, She twisted away from the policeman and ran for the door into the street. He caught her easily, pinioned her flailing arms to her sides and half carried her into the lounge. 'This the little lass you were talking about?' he asked Tim, breathlessly.

Tim nodded silently. She looked so little, so wretchedly afraid . . .

'What were you doing?' the policeman asked her. She said nothing. He let her go, but moved between her and the door. She stood, trembling and hanging her head.

Mrs Hoggart said pityingly, 'No one's going to hurt you, dear. Were you looking for Tim?'

No answer.

'She doesn't like being asked questions,' Tim said.

Mrs Hoggart looked at the policeman who shrugged his shoulders in a helpless way. 'You speak to her, Tim,' she said. 'Tell her not to be frightened.'

He looked at her. 'Perdita . . . it's all right . . . don't be scared.'

She gave no sign of having heard him. Except for the fluttery rise and fall of her chest, she was motionless as a statue.

Tim said, 'They've caught Mr Jones. They know he's a bad man. You know he is, too, because he left us in the cave and he stole all those jewels. He gave you one, didn't he?'

She remained silent and still.

Tim drew a deep breath and glanced at the policeman. *Go on, you're doing fine*, his expression said. Tim felt suddenly ashamed, he wasn't sure why. After all, it was right to help the police, wasn't it? He was sure of this, quite sure of it, all the same, his voice was slow and reluctant. 'He gave you that diamond, one of those he had in the box, do you remember? The night he came up to see Mr Smith . . .'

She lifted her head now and looked at him with a strange, blank stare as if he were speaking in a language she didn't under-stand. *A little wild thing, half-crazed*. . . . Remembering what Mr Tarbutt had told the policeman, Tim thought that, at this moment, it looked pretty true. He felt, all at once, impatient with her. Why – she looked plumb daft – *loony*. And, in a way, that reflected on *him*, didn't it? He had repeated what she had told him, hadn't he? As gospel truth. So now it looked – well, it just looked as if he was the sort of boy who would listen to any wild sort of tale from a girl who wasn't quite right in the head. As if he was a fool, easily taken in . . .

He said, 'You did tell me all those things. Didn't you?' She flinched back as he advanced on her and he controlled himself. He went on, more gently, 'It's all right, you can tell now. There's only my Mum here, and she's O.K. and this man who's a policeman, so it's all right to tell him. People ought to tell things, it's a person's duty.' He hesitated and then thought of a better way to persuade her – one that would almost certainly work with Janey, and all girls were the same. Contrary. 'All right,' he said. '*Don't*, then. If you really don't want to tell him, I don't suppose it matters much. I don't even know he'd be interested! He knows all about it, anyway. About Mr Jones being a jewel robber and . . . and . . .' Suddenly remembering what the policeman had said earlier, he glanced at him nervously, but he responded with an almost imperceptible nod. '. . . and about Mr Smith being one, too,' Tim finished triumphantly. 'So you see, you needn't bother to . . .'

She gave a little, gasping cry, and ran.

The policeman could have stopped her quite easily. Instead, he moved aside and stood with his arms folded. She went into the sun parlour and they heard the sudden howl of wind as she pulled open the door on to the street. Tim would have run after her, but the policeman said, in a voice that commanded obedience, 'No, Tim. Let her go.'

'It's dark,' Mrs Hoggart said, looking worried. 'We ought to go after her. A child like that, alone . . .'

'I wonder if she is,' the policeman said.

Tim turned on his mother. 'Oh, don't *fuss*. She's all right – Skua's not like London.'

He made this protest automatically: his mind was occupied with something else. He looked at the policeman and said, in a voice that had suddenly gone quiet. 'What I said – that was slander. Since you said there's no proof he's done anything . . .'

The policeman looked at him thoughtfully, fingering the mole on his cheek.

Tim went on, 'If she tells Mr Smith . . .' He caught his breath. 'Can you be sent to prison for slander?'

The policeman laughed. 'I shouldn't worry, Tim. An innocent man will hardly worry himself over what one child says to another. Look a fine fool if he did, wouldn't he?'

'But suppose he isn't innocent,' Tim said slowly.

'Maybe this is one way of finding out,' the policeman said.

14

GOLF CLUBS AND LOBSTERS

'I DIDN'T mean to carry tales,' Perdita said. 'It was just that Janey didn't run away from me, the way the others always do.'

'Poor little witch,' Mr Smith said.

His tone was unexpectedly gentle. It was the first time he had spoken since she had stumbled back into the car to tell him what she knew – or, rather, to repeat parrot-fashion what Tim had said. In spite of Tim's explanation in the cave, she did not really understand what Mr Smith was supposed to have done wrong. How could she? She had lived all her life on this lonely island, with only Annie MacLaren for company. She knew where the buzzards nested and how to get close to the red deer without frightening them, but she knew nothing about thieves and jewellers' shops.

After she had finished, Mr Smith had sat still a minute, staring straight in front of him. Then he had turned the car and driven back to Luinpool in a silence so absolute that Perdita thought he must have forgotten her. But when they reached the house, and she had opened and closed the yard gate, he had waited for her by the back door, picked her up in his arms as she stumbled with tiredness, and carried her into the kitchen. He had sent Annie to bed before he drove down to Skuaphort, telling her not to worry, he would look after the child, and the warm kitchen was dark except for one oil lamp, turned low, and the yellow light from the fire. He sat Perdita on the settle and knelt in front of her to take off her boots. She looked down at his bent head, thinking confusedly about all that had happened, and about her own part in it, and tried to say she was sorry, in the only way she knew.

When she had spoken, he sat back on his heels. 'Poor little

witch,' he repeated, and sighed. 'Still, what's done is done, there's no mending it.'

He spoke so drearily that although he didn't seem angry with her, as she had been afraid he would be, a tear rolled down Perdita's cheek.

'Oh, for heaven's sake, don't start blubbing,' he said, on the edge of anger, and then, controlling himself, 'Witches don't cry, you know I've told you that before.'

'I'm not a witch,' Perdita sobbed. 'Not any more. I lost my Powers like you said I would.'

'Pity!' Mr Smith gave a short, unamused laugh. 'A spot of second sight would come in useful just now.'

He got to his feet and stood, staring into the fire, forgetting the child for the moment in thoughts of his own perilous situation. How much did the police really know? How much was bluff – or guesswork? Mr Smith was not a stupid man, and it crossed his mind as he stood there, musing, that it was possible that this was a trap – that the police knew nothing, had no real evidence against him and were hoping that he would lose his head and do something to give himself away. He frowned into the fire. It was possible, but he could not rely upon it. If Mr Jones had really been caught, red-handed with the jewels, he would certainly tell the police all he knew – turn Queen's Evidence, perhaps, in the hope that he would get a lighter sentence. There was no honour among thieves. He would say he had not wanted to take part in the robbery, that he had been talked into it. He would say he was a weak man. Well, *that* was true enough, Mr Smith thought, suddenly smiling. He had watched Mr Jones for several weeks before approaching him with his proposition; watched him lunching with his cronies, shopping with his children at weekends. He was the sort of man who always stays after he has said he must go, who protests but still has a second cup of coffee or another beer, who always gives in to his children when they pester him for ice-cream in the street . . .

Mr Smith stopped smiling. In the circumstances, Mr Jones's weakness of character was not really amusing.

He looked at Perdita. She was sitting on the settle, tears running silently down her face.

'Still crying?' he said impatiently. 'Whatever for?'

'Because Annie says you're going away.'

His irritation left him. He had led a lonely, roaming existence all his life and no one had been sorry when he had left a place before. This thought gave him a strange feeling – strange, but not disagreeable.

'Will you miss me?' he asked.

She looked at him with swollen eyes. '*Are* you going?'

'I think a sea voyage might be good for my health at the moment.' He watched her thoughtfully. If they had used her to trap him, *he* could use her too, to throw them off the scent a little. 'Just round the islands,' he said. 'Maybe a little trip to Trull…'

'Are you going to South America, like Mr Jones?'

'Why should you think that?' He smiled at her. 'No, just round the islands. A bit of fishing, maybe…'

She said, 'Can I come too? You said I could, once.'

He said nothing for a minute and then his face softened. He said, 'Maybe…' He hesitated. 'Shut your eyes and lie down on the settle.'

'Will you tell me about it? Like you did before?'

He nodded and she stretched out obediently on the cushions, half closing her eyes.

Mr Smith said in a low, soothing voice, 'Perhaps we'll go farther than the islands. We'll leave on the morning tide and sail south, perhaps, on and on till we get to…'

'Africa,' she said. 'Africa. That's where I'd like to go.'

'Africa, then. We'll sail down the coast of Africa and sometimes we'll stop and go ashore and buy pineapples and papayas and…'

'And a parrot,' she said with a little yawn. 'Don't forget the parrot…'

'A green one,' he said, 'with purple tail feathers and a yellow patch on his head and bits of red here and there and a beak like a bill-hook. We'll teach him to talk and he'll live with us on the boat and we'll teach him to tell the time so we don't have to look at our watches when we want to know, just ask him and he'll tell us. I never heard of a parrot could tell the time before, but I daresay we'll be lucky and find an exceptional one. We might even train him to catch fish for us, like a heron. They do that in some parts of the world, and I don't see why a properly brought up parrot should be less smart than an old heron. Our parrot will be a very special parrot altogether. People will send from all over the world and ask to buy him, but of course we'll always say no. Of course, we'll have to think of a name for him, won't we?' He paused. 'Can you think of a name?'

There was no answer. She had fallen asleep, smiling.

He took the oil lamp and went quietly out of the room and up the stairs. When he returned a few minutes later, he was wearing an oilskin and sea boots and carrying the canvas grip he had kept packed for just this sort of emergency, as he had kept his boat ready, supplied with fuel and tinned food. He crossed the settle and stood beside the sleeping child. One hand supported her flushed cheek, the other was holding something through her dress. Mr Smith bent over her and pulled gently at the string round her neck until the diamond came into view. He held his breath while she flung her arm wide, muttering, but then she relaxed again, her fingers loosely curled over the place on her flat little chest where the stone had been hidden. He took a knife from his pocket and stayed still a minute, watching her face, before he cut the string in two places and slipped the stone in his pocket.

'Good-bye witch,' he said, and went out of the back door, closing it softly behind him.

The sound of the car starting up disturbed her, but not enough to wake her fully. She just jerked a little as if she had

had a falling dream, but then she went properly to sleep again and slept deeply, not stirring until some time after three o'clock in the morning, when the fire died and the room grew cold and the old cockerel, roosting on the pile of peat in the yard, let out his first sleepy, dawn crow.

Tim woke at about the same time. Like Perdita he had slept deeply at first, from exhaustion, but the moment he opened his eyes he was fully awake, his mind active and crammed full, as if it had been working hard all the time his body had been asleep.

For a short while he lay still, listening to the hollow thunder of the wind. It was not morning yet, but, because the nights were short on Skua, the darkness was already paling outside the window. Restless, he tossed in his bed and made a groaning sound, hoping Janey would wake up so he could talk to her. But she slept soundly on.

He felt he must talk, or his mind would burst. So he whispered aloud, 'What did he do with the jewels, then? If he didn't have them on him when he was caught? Gave them to Mr Campbell? *I* wouldn't have done that. Even if I trusted him, it wouldn't be safe, the police might have searched him, too. Perhaps he didn't have them with him at all. He must have known, after he knocked Dad down, the police would be looking for him. If I'd been him I wouldn't have taken them with me, just in case. I'd have left them hidden somewhere. Somewhere good and safe . . .'

He stopped and sighed. Last night, before he went to bed, he had asked the policeman what he thought had happened to the jewels but he had just shrugged his shoulders, and then, as if he didn't want to discuss Mr Jones or Mr Smith any more, had told Tim how thieves sometimes hid their loot in the oddest places. One he knew had planted roses: when the police dug up his rose garden, they found silver – cigarette boxes, candlesticks – buried beneath each rose.

'How did you know where to look?' Tim had asked.

'We'd been watching him. As it happened, this man had never shown any interest in his garden before. So when he did, it was out of character, something that didn't quite fit in. D'you see?'

'Like Mr Jones bringing golf clubs to Skua? That was odd, because there isn't a golf course, and if he'd really wanted to play he'd have found that out, wouldn't he? Before he bought new golf clubs? So it looks as if he just thought there probably was a course and he brought the clubs as a sort of disguise in case anyone should wonder what he was coming to Skua *for*.'

The policeman had smiled approvingly and said he was a sharp lad, and Tim had swelled with pride. If only his father had heard that!

Now, smiling to himself, he spoke into the darkness. 'You see, Dad, little things *are* important. Even if they don't always seem it. It's like doing a jigsaw puzzle. All the little bits don't mean much on their own, till you fit them together to make a pattern. I expect, if I think about it, there are quite a number of other things I've noticed, even if I don't quite see where they fit in yet . . .'

What, though? What little thing could there be, that the police didn't know already? About Mr Jones or Mr Smith? What did *he* know about Mr Smith? Nothing peculiar, really, that he hadn't told the policeman. He was just a man who kept himself to himself except that sometimes he went lobster fishing with Mr Campbell, though Perdita said Mr Smith didn't like lobsters.

Lobsters! Suddenly, Tim sat up in bed. 'Janey,' he said, so excited suddenly that he could not keep it to himself. 'Janey – wake up!'

She rolled over on her back with a little, gruffling snort, and put her thumb in her mouth.

Tim looked at her indecisively. His mother had said she was worn out, poor child, and he must be careful not to disturb her.

But he had to tell someone. Mum! Mum wouldn't mind being woken up. This was the sort of thing that was bound to interest her. He got out of bed and ran from the room.

Mrs Hoggart was asleep. He tugged at her arm to waken her and she stirred sleepily. 'Wha . . .?' she began, and then sat bolt upright with a little cry. The room was suddenly illuminated with yellow light and the light was followed by a loud crack, like a big firework exploding.

Tim rushed to the window. Another flare went up. 'Mum,' he shouted, 'Mum! There's a boat on the rocks!'

15

ON THE ROCKS

WITHIN about ten minutes, it seemed, the little town was alive, the jetty crowded with people – men, women, children, even babies-in-arms, their faces still round and solemn with sleep. A few men were fully dressed in oilskins and sea boots but most people wore only a coat, hastily thrown over their night-clothes. In the hotel, only Mrs Hoggart stayed indoors, watching from her bedroom window, because Janey still slept, in spite of the commotion. Mrs Hoggart would have kept Tim with her but, guessing this, he had wisely gone before she could tell him to stay.

At first Tim could see nothing – nor could anyone else. A heavy mass of black cloud obscured the sea and harbour. For a little it was all Tim could do to stand against the wind which rushed like something solid into his mouth and up his nostrils. His eyes streamed with water – his own, salty tears mingling with the spray that dashed up against the sides of the jetty. Then, suddenly, the horizon began to clear. The furious wind seemed to sweep the sky, driving the black mass of cloud before it as if rolling up a curtain. Almost at once, a cry went up. The boat – clearly seen now, in the greying light – was caught on the rocks beyond the harbour. The heavy sea seemed to lift it rhythmically: each time the great waves receded, they left the little boat smashed farther and farther on its side.

After the first two flares there had been no more. There was no sign of life on the boat, which was not identified at first. Then, 'It's the *Asti*,' a man shouted. 'Mr Smith's boat.'

'Madness,' another said. '*Madness*.' Terrified and excited at the same time, Tim pushed his way among the crowd and heard them conjecture that Mr Smith must have left the bay where he kept his boat – the next round the coast – and, discovering that he couldn't handle her, had tried to run into Skuaphort for shelter instead of making for the open sea where he would, at least, have had 'sea room' and a chance of survival. 'What was the fool thinking of?' one old fisherman said. To enter Skuaphort from the far side of the loch was dangerous in any weather: with this sea and wind driving any boat on to the partly submerged rocks, it was utter folly.

A boat was manned but it was impossible to get it out of the harbour: beyond the sheltering arm of the jetty, the sea rose up like a wall. Since rescue from the sea was clearly impossible, the people left the jetty and made their way round Loch Kinnit to the point on the opposite side from the town, where a small group of men had already gathered on the beach. From this point, the wicked line of rocks ran out, jagged and black. The sea cracked against them with a sound like cannon fire and from time to time they disappeared completely, under a level surface of yellow froth.

The townspeople gathered on a little bluff and watched the men on the beach. Ropes had been brought. One fisherman waded into the black water which was, at one second, only ankle deep, and the next rose chest high as a wave swelled in. He made for the rocks. The distance was nothing, but the terrible sea made it a desperate journey, and, though he struggled hard, he had to be dragged back, face and hands cut and bleeding, before he had managed to get even a third of the way to the wrecked boat. Another man volunteered at once, and his wife, a plump woman who wore an old army greatcoat over her nightdress, jumped down off the bluff and clung to him, weeping and shouting. He was not to go. He was not to leave her. He would be drowned as her father had been. The tears streamed down her face. Tim felt that he ought not to watch her and was ashamed because he could not tear his eyes away. In the end, others intervened and said the woman was right. 'There's not a thing anyone can do,' one man said.

The words were ominous like a tolling bell. People fell silent, huddling together in the dawn light. The boat was lower in the water now and could only be seen occasionally. The mast, its stays long since parted, had snapped in two, like a twig.

'Wheelhouse gone,' someone said, and a kind of corporate sigh, or groan, ran through the group of watchers.

For a little while, no one moved, or spoke, except in undertones. Even the littlest children were silent now, huddling beside their parents or staring round-eyed, from the shelter of their arms.

'Is there any chance?' a low voice said. Tim turned. The policeman was standing behind him, his red and white pyjama jacket visible under his overcoat. He had spoken to Mr Tarbutt, who was shaking his head.

'He's gone now, for certain. Cabin'll be full of water.'

The policeman swore softly. He must have gone very pale, Tim thought, because the dark mole on his cheek seemed to stand out more than before. Then he said, 'I never thought he'd be such a fool – on a night like this . . .'

'She's breaking up,' someone shouted, and the whole crowd seemed to surge forward in unison, like a wave.

There was no sign of the broken mast now. A bigger wave than any that had gone before, had turned the boat completely over, exposing her white hull.

It was then that Tim saw Perdita. She was down on the beach, standing some way away from a group of fishermen. The instant he set eyes upon her, she began to run. Tim slipped over the side of the bluff, landing on the rocky beach with a jar that sent an arrow of pain shooting through his sprained ankle. He shouted her name with all his strength, but she didn't turn.

She was making straight for the rocks. All eyes were fixed on the foundering ship and no one had noticed her except Tim. She was waist deep in water before Tim could get to the nearest

man and grab his sleeve. 'She'll drown,' he shouted. 'Oh look
– she'll drown . . .'

The man looked bewildered and then let out a hoarse cry as
he saw where Tim was pointing. She was clinging to a rock –
clinging for her life as a green wave curled over her. She disappeared, and then, as the sea sucked back, they saw she was
still there, small, hunched, the pale blur of her face turned towards the shore. The fisherman shook Tim from his arm and
ran. He was in the sea and almost at the rocks by the time the
next wave came and the rest of the watchers had seen the
danger. 'Rope – get a rope,' someone shouted. Then a woman
screamed – a high, level sound like a train whistle.

The second wave had swept the child off the rock. There was
no sign of her.

Tim felt deathly sick. The beach was a pandemonium of
cries and running men. Bulky figures rushed past him, shutting
off his view of the sea: one knocked him flying. He fell on the
beach and lay there, sand and salt in his mouth and terrible
thoughts in his mind. *This was all his fault.* If he had not talked
to the policeman, if he had not talked to *her*, last night . . .

Someone took hold of his arm, and jerked him to his feet.
He looked up, saw the policeman, and then felt as if something
had exploded in his head. He thumped the policeman in the
stomach with his free hand and shouted, 'Get away, get
away, I *hate* you . . .'

'Steady on, old chap,' the policeman said. And then, 'It's all
right, boy, it's all right . . .'

He held Tim's shoulders and twisted him roughly so that he
could see the fisherman stumbling in the water, holding her in
his arms. Willing hands helped them ashore and laid the child
on the beach.

Her hair streamed on the pebbles like dark seaweed. She lay
on her face and Mr Tarbutt knelt beside her. Tim would have
run to them but the policeman took his hand and held him
back, while a knot of people gathered round, obscuring his

view. The policeman held Tim's hand very tight and it seemed to the boy that ages passed. His first rush of glad relief when he had seen she was safe had subsided, leaving him in the grip of a bleak and terrible despair. She was dead – dead, and it was his fault. He was quite convinced that she was drowned, that they would never revive her, when a woman cried out that she was breathing.

Instantly, a wave of relief swept through the crowd, spreading in ripples of movement, even of half-hysterical laughter as the people shouted the good news to each other. Someone brought blankets and she was lifted, rolled up like a cocoon with her head against Mr Tarbutt's broad shoulder.

'Don't cry,' the policeman said to Tim. 'She's all right now.'

Tim had not realized he was crying until he lifted his hand and felt his face was wet. By the time the policeman had produced a handkerchief to dry his eyes, Tim had recovered sufficiently from his despair to be ashamed of his babyish behaviour and to insist that he wasn't crying, it was just that his face was wet with spray.

'Nothing to be ashamed of if you were,' the policeman said.

The people of Skuaphort straggled back home. The morning light reddened their faces, which were strained and grave. A life had been saved, but another had almost certainly been lost, and, thinking of Mr Smith, they thought of others, too: of fathers, husbands, brothers, sons. There were few families on Skua that had not lost someone to the sea.

Only the young children were not oppressed by the general feeling of sadness and mourning. Earlier, they had been frightened and clung to their parents: now the drama was over, some five or six of them gathered together and began to whisper and giggle. No one took any notice of them, and, by the time the procession had reached the town, their voices became louder and less restrained.

'She's a witch for certain,' said one fat little seven-year-old. '*I'm* not scared, though . . .'

'You'd better be, Will McBaine,' his sister said. 'Or she'll turn you into a toad.'

'Or a crow. A big, black, flappy crow . . .'

The little boy's face went red. 'She will *not*, then. Alistair Campbell threw a stone at her, and she didn't turn him into anything at all.'

His voice piped up clear in the morning. Several women turned to look at the children. Suddenly one of them turned very red and said in a loud voice, 'That's enough!' She rushed at her own small daughter and gave her a hearty smack. For a moment the child was silent, dumb with astonishment. Then she opened her mouth and bawled like a calf. 'And that's what the rest should be getting,' her mother cried, looking defiantly and angrily round her.

The other women glanced at each other. None of them really believed the little girl from Luinpool was a witch, but they had let their children say so, not bothering to correct them, either out of idleness, or because the superstitious nonsense amused them. Now, shame stirred in them, and, before they could take to their heels, the astonished children found themselves seized, and shaken or spanked – not very hard, perhaps, because their mothers were uncomfortably aware that they were as much at fault as their children – but hard enough to make them cry. Their wailing rose to the pink, morning sky, and Mr Tarbutt, entering the hotel with his burden, smiled to himself, rather grimly.

Perdita was put to bed. Mrs Tarbutt, who had been waiting with hot water bottles and warm milk, came downstairs a little later and said the lassie was sleeping now and that Mr Tarbutt had better go up to Luinpool for Annie MacLaren.

Tim and the policeman got the remains of the hot milk which had sugar and brandy in it.

They drank in silence. Then the policeman cleared his throat. 'Don't blame yourself, Tim,' he said.

Tim put his empty cup down on the table and stared at it.

The policeman said, 'You did your best. It was you saw the fire and sounded the alarm. No one could have done anything in that sea.'

Tim remained obstinately silent. But, as he sat there glumly staring into space, he remembered what he had been thinking about before he saw the first flare go up from the boat. For a moment he struggled with himself. He didn't want to talk to the policeman any more, but he couldn't bear to keep this interesting piece of deduction to himself, either.

In the end he said, very grudgingly, 'I think I know where Mr Smith kept his jewels. In the cave.' The policeman smiled, and Tim went a little red. 'It's not just a guess. You see, he didn't like lobsters.'

The policeman raised one eyebrow.

Tim said, 'He went lobster fishing, and there's no real sport in that, not like trout or salmon, so there must have been some other reason. I think it was because he wanted an excuse to go down to the cave whenever he wanted, and if he was going fishing, no one would think it funny.'

The policeman was stroking his stubbly chin with the palm of his hand. 'It's an interesting theory. Quite a likely one, perhaps, though I don't see that we can ever prove it. Never mind.' He smiled, and his eyes were amused and friendly. 'You know, young man, if it should ever take your fancy, you'd make a very useful detective, some day.'

Though this was something Tim had always longed to hear, for some reason it gave him no particular pleasure now.

He said, rather coldly, 'I think I'd rather be a botanist, like my father. Not so many people get hurt.'

16

A NEEDLE IN A HAYSTACK

TIM had honestly believed, when his mother sent him to bed that morning, that he would never sleep again. But he slept all day and woke in the evening too drowsy to swallow more than half a glass of milk and a digestive biscuit before his eyes closed and Mrs Hoggart put out the light. When he finally woke up properly, halfway through the following afternoon, the policeman had left and his father had arrived on a hired motor boat.

Mr Hoggart had been allowed out of hospital that morning and was pale, but recovered. He was gently humble with his son and did not once comment on Tim's romantic imagination. Instead, he encouraged Tim to tell him all that had happened and even speculated himself upon where Mr Jones's share of the loot might be. 'The most likely thing, I would think, is that he gave the jewels to Mr Campbell – and there's no sign of him yet. I'm afraid the chances are no one will ever find them.'

'Because there weren't any? That's what you really think isn't it?' Tim's voice was too indifferent to be rude. It sounded simply as if he no longer cared much, one way or the other. He was quiet for a minute, leaning back listlessly against the pillows and staring out of the window, and then he said, 'What happened about the wreck?'

His father hesitated. Then he told Tim that salvage operations had begun on the boat, but so far they had yielded nothing. Tim's face remained calm. Mr Hoggart cleared his throat and said that Mr Smith's body had not yet been recovered, and, if he had had any jewels with him, they had almost certainly gone to the bottom of the sea. As for Perdita's diamond, Mr Hoggart went on, she had it no longer. The words, *if she ever did have it,* trembled on the tip of his tongue but he refrained from speaking them aloud, saying only, 'I expect she lost it in the sea, poor child.'

Then he fell silent, thinking not about the diamond but about the little girl who had not, Mrs Hoggart had told him, spoken once since her rescue, only clung dumbly to Annie MacLaren until the old woman had asked Mr Tarbutt to take them back to Luinpool and to leave them there in peace.

'Will they be able to stay there?' Tim asked suddenly. 'I mean it was . . .' He swallowed and turned pale. 'It was *his* house, wasn't it?'

Mr Hoggart pushed his glasses up on his nose and looked at his son anxiously. He had tried to talk about the wreck in an ordinary, matter-of-fact way, because it had seemed better to talk and to accept what had happened than to pretend nothing had. Now he wondered if he had been wrong. Tim was not to blame for what had happened to Mr Smith – or only in such a roundabout way that no sensible person would count it as blame. But was Tim sensible? Mr Hoggart reminded himself that he had often thought he was not, and been impatient with him because of it. Remembering this made him nervous. He wanted to talk to Tim about Mr Smith but did not know how to begin. So instead, he smiled brightly and said in an unnaturally cheery voice, 'We thought we might go on a picnic tomorrow. Janey wants to go back to Carlin's Cave – to show us the scene of her triumph! We've got a day before the steamer comes and Mr Tarbutt says he'll take us in a boat. Would you like that?'

'I don't mind.' Tim spoke about as enthusiastically as if his father had suggested a trip to the natural history museum. Then he looked at him. 'You don't have to cheer me up. I mean, I know it wasn't really my fault about Mr Smith – at least, I know it in my head. What you call *sensibly*. But it doesn't feel like that in my . . . my *inside*, and I don't suppose it ever will. Not for a long time, anyway.' He paused. 'But what I asked you – I mean, I really wanted to *know*. What'll happen to Perdita, if he's dead?'

Mr Hoggart took out his handkerchief and blew his nose. He said – it seemed for no particular reason – 'I'm sorry, Tim.' And then, 'She'll be all right. At least, from what Mr Tarbutt says, she'll have a roof over her head.'

'Mr Smith left a will,' Annie MacLaren said. She sat in the kitchen at Luinpool and Perdita lay on the settle opposite her. 'That policeman found it yesterday when he was up here turning everything upside down and higgledy-piggledy. It seems the house is yours, lady.'

Perdita did not appear to have heard. She was staring into the fire.

Annie MacLaren sighed. 'At least we'll have a roof over our heads, even if it leaks in places. And we've got my pension and the little bit I've put by.'

There was silence except for the hiss of the fire and the tick of the clock in the corner.

'I had a long talk with Mrs Hoggart,' Annie said. 'She's a nice woman and very well educated. She says you should go to school. Here first, and then the big school on Trull. Will you like that?'

A faint interest stirred in the child's eyes, but vanished almost at once.

Annie looked at her, her heart wrung. 'There's been a lot of things sent. Mr Duncan sent up a nice chicken, and butter, and a pound of tea. And the Findlay boy came up this morning with a packet of chocolate.' There had been other gifts too, left secretly at the back door or sent in the back of Duncan's van, when he delivered the chicken. Perdita had shown no interest in any of them. She had eaten nothing, seemed to want nothing, except that Annie should stay with her. The old woman had sat up all night, sleepless on a chair, while Perdita had moaned and tossed in her narrow bed. Tired now, and distressed by the child's lack of response, tears welled up in the old woman's eyes and slipped down her soft, pouchy cheeks.

For a moment Perdita stayed where she was, looking away and frowning as if pretending to herself there was nothing wrong. Then she gave a little sigh, slipped off the settle and went over to Annie. She put her arms round her – or, rather, round as much of her as she could manage, since Annie was a big woman – and whispered in her ear. 'Will I make you a cup of tea, Annie? And a nice bit of toast, at the fire?'

Mrs Hoggart and Janey arrived just as Perdita had finished making the tea and setting out cups on a tray. Annie's hands flew to untie her apron while Perdita went to the door. She went reluctantly, only because Annie had told her to, and stood with her eyes on the ground while Mrs Hoggart asked her how she was, and told her that she and Janey had come to see if she would like to go on a picnic tomorrow. Would she like that? Perdita did not answer and Mrs Hoggart went on encouragingly. If she would like to come, they had thought of doing something rather especially exciting . . .

Perdita shuffled her feet and scowled. For Annie's sake, she had made an effort to talk and make tea, but she still felt very stiff and strange, rather as if she had a lump of ice inside her instead of a heart. And she was not used to loud, cheerful people like Mrs Hoggart with bright, bustling voices – though, in fact, poor Mrs Hoggart's voice became a good deal less bright as she looked at this unwelcoming little girl who scowled and scowled and said nothing. She was about to say, 'Well, dear, another day, then?' and beat a hasty retreat, when Janey spoke.

'Aren't you going to ask us in? It's absolutely horribly rude, when visitors come, to keep them waiting on the doorstep.'

'Oh Janey, you mustn't . . .' Mrs Hoggart began, and then stopped, because Perdita was smiling.

It was a shy, lop-sided smile, and it vanished almost at once, but it was still a smile. She said, 'If you like, you can come in and have a cup of tea.'

After that it was all right – or almost all right. They had tea and Annie made toast by the range fire and spread it generously with Mr Duncan's butter while they talked. At least, while Janey talked. She ate more toast than anyone else and still had time to talk much more. She told Annie how they had been left in the cave and how they would almost certainly have died, if she had not been clever enough to find the way out. 'It was terribly clever of me,' she said admiringly, after she had told the story for the second time. 'If it hadn't been for me, we would have been skeletons by now, I expect, just our poor bones lying there, like the sheep skulls. I was a heroine, wasn't I, Perdita?'

Directly addressed, Perdita seemed to shrink into herself. She had not spoken since she had invited them in, Mrs Hoggart realized, just crouched still and quiet on a footstool beside Annie MacLaren's chair. Now she glanced nervously in Mrs Hoggart's direction and whispered, very low, 'It was magic, Annie. I couldn't see, it was pitch, but *she* could. She has the Second Sight.'

'Not as good as you,' Janey said. 'I told my Dad about you and I told him Tim said it wasn't true about second sight, and I asked Dad if it *was*, and he said, well, perhaps it was, in a way. He said he didn't believe in witches himself, but he was sure some people were special, all the same. Blind ones like me and girls who've been alone a lot, like you. He said we've learned to see and hear things other people don't have time to, because they're always too busy just looking and playing. Dad says people like you and me – well – it's as if we'd grown an extra piece of ourselves that other people don't have . . .' She swallowed her last piece of toast and added, kindly, 'I expect, if you'd really tried, Perdita, you could have found your way out of the cave by yourself.' She did not really believe this, but it brought the conversation back to her own stupendous achievement. 'That's where we're going tomorrow, to the cave. So Mum and Dad can see just what I did and how hard it was. You will come, won't you? We're going to take an extra special picnic.'

Perdita stared in horror – as if, Mrs Hoggart thought, she had been invited to accompany Janey into a lion's den – before shaking her head violently. Then, remembering Janey could not see her, she said, 'No thank you,' and began to blush.

'She's not used to a lot of people,' Annie said.

'She's used to me and Tim. And we won't be a lot. Only five. Our family and Mr Tarbutt.'

'Five people at once is a lot for her,' Annie said.

Janey scowled. 'She'll have to get used to more people than five when she goes to school. So she might as well start now.'

'That's enough, dear,' her mother said, seeing Perdita's miserable look and the painful colour rising in her cheeks. 'Perhaps she'll think it over tonight and decide to come tomorrow.'

But she didn't come. They waited for nearly an hour after the time Mrs Hoggart had told Annie they would be leaving the hotel, but there was no sign of her. Mr Tarbutt offered to drive up and fetch her but Mrs Hoggart said that would be unkind. 'If she'd wanted to come, she'd have come. The child's shy and – well – upset, I imagine. After all, she's had a terrible time, these last few days.

Mr Hoggart glanced at Tim and gave his wife a warning frown. Tim gave no sign of having heard, but when they were in the boat and heading seaward, out of Loch Kinnit, he said suddenly, 'I expect it's *me* she doesn't want to see. I expect she thinks it's all my fault.'

Mr Hoggart put his hand over his son's and pressed it. Then he said, 'Maybe she thinks it's her's. Have you thought of that?'

The sea was calm and solid. Mr Tarbutt's boat skimmed over it. The outboard motor spluttered and spray blew in their faces. He let Janey sit in the stern and hold the tiller, explaining how she could steer by the feel of the wind on her cheek. 'I love the sea, I love the sea,' she chanted. 'I'm going to be a sailor when I grow up.'

They rounded the point of Loch Kinnit and crossed the bay where the great rock reared up like a castle. They could see the path round the headland, a hair-thin line against the cliff. Mr Tarbutt slowed the motor and put his hand over Janey's to steer the boat into harbour at Carlin's Cave. They passed Mr Campbell's green glass lobster floats, bobbing above his pots.

'I wonder if they'll ever find him,' Tim said half to himself.

'Campbell?' Mr Tarbutt grinned. 'They'll have a job – if he doesn't want to be found. And I'd be surprised if anyone was really bothered to try. Why should they? Unless those jewels of yours turn up, young man.'

His eyes twinkled at Tim in a friendly, but amused and sceptical way. Tim looked at his mother and father and saw they were smiling too. He turned away and stared moodily at the approaching shore. The outboard motor cut out and the boat slipped quietly into the little harbour. Mr Tarbutt tied up and helped Mrs Hoggart with the picnic basket. Mr Hoggart carried Janey over the rocks to the beach.

Tim followed them slowly. No one believed him, he thought. Janey did, but she was only small, she would believe a lie if he told her. Perhaps his mother did, but she was not really *interested*, now he and Janey were safe and his father well and they were all together again. Nor was his father: though he had made a show of being interested, to please him, all he really wanted was to forget about the whole business. He had told the police that as far as he was concerned, he would prefer them not to press the charge against Mr Jones. 'Give him the benefit of the doubt,' Tim had heard him say to his mother as he passed their bedroom door that morning. 'I admit I thought he'd pushed me deliberately, but it's all so hazy in my mind now – it might well have been an accident, as he says. And, as for the business of the children and the cave . . .'

He had lowered his voice then, and Tim could not hear what

his next words were, but his imagination supplied them. *We've only Tim's word for that, and you know what he is.* And then his mother had said, 'Well, it doesn't really matter, I suppose. It's all over now.'

All over now. As they explored the cave, the comforting light of torches and lanterns showing them the dangerous way Janey had led them to safety, the words whispered over and over inside Tim's head.

All over now – for Mr Smith? Tim flinched inside him and fixed his mind on the policeman. *He* had said he believed him, but he had also said what he believed wasn't evidence. Was it even evidence, the fact that Mr Smith had run away? They might guess Perdita had warned him, but would they ever *know*? Remembering the way she had behaved that night at the hotel, Tim thought it unlikely that she would ever talk to a stranger. *Of course, she might tell me,* he thought, and then, suddenly, *perhaps that's why she didn't come today, she knows I'd ask questions and she hates that . . .*

In front of him, his father was holding a lantern high and Janey was saying, 'This is the place where I shouted and Tim was frightened.'

Tim felt a faint indignation, but it died almost at once. He stumped down the tunnel after the others, and crossed the ravine by the wall. Then the stairway. He lingered there, as the others went on, into the cavern. Then he switched out his own torch and stood in the dark. This was where he had heard the men talking. Suddenly, he could hear every word clear, like ghost voices, mocking him. *Smithie can look after himself . . . he's good at that. . . . The whole idea was his. . . . And then getting me to go stealing that kid's ruby . . . Risky to leave it, he said. . . .*

He *had* heard it. He hadn't dreamed it. Or made it up, as he was certain his father believed. Oh – it was a horrible, nightmarish feeling, to know something was true, and yet no one believed you. Tim shivered. *The kid's ruby. Risky to leave it.* Risky? Why? Because they might have realized in the end that it really was a ruby, and other people might come search-ing? And because Mr Smith didn't want people searching in the cave because it was a convenient place to leave the stolen treasure? A place where he could come and go quite openly, on the face of it lobster fishing with Mr Campbell, but really to look at the jewels, counting them like a miser, sometimes taking a few to sell, or to give Mr Jones his share . . .

And, at one of those times, one tiny ruby had slipped through his fingers, and Tim had found it . . .

Tim felt sick in his stomach. It was so obvious to him. But there was no way of proving it. He began to stumble back along the tunnel, not waiting for the others. If Mr Smith had hidden the jewels here, wouldn't he have taken them, before he set sail? Or would he have left them, thinking to slip into the little harbour and collect them another time, when the hue and cry had died down?

He came out into the main cave. The walls rose high above his head, and, beyond the mouth of the tunnel, the cave went back, into darkness. He walked away from the beach, deeper into the cliff. It was an enormous cave – *vast*. There were hun-dreds of boulders, hundreds of rock pools, hundreds of ledges, crevices, hiding places . . .

He lost his footing and slipped into a rock pool scraping his knee, and was glad of the excuse to whimper a little. He peered between the boulders and up at the high, black walls, aimlessly, despairingly . . .

The others emerged from the tunnel. Mrs Hoggart, who had not enjoyed this expedition, was looking slightly green. 'I think I could do with my lunch,' she said, and went quickly towards the light and the sunshine. Janey and Mr Tarbutt went with her. Mr Hoggart walked towards the back of the cave and saw the light of Tim's torch and then Tim himself, scrambling desperately over the great boulders, thrusting his hand into cracks and crevices, looking hopelessly around him . . .

Mr Hoggart watched him for a minute. Then he said, 'You'd need an army, Tim, to search this place.'

Tim paused in his frantic search. He tried to speak, but a sob choked him.

Mr Hoggart said gently, 'I know all boys like to think of finding hidden treasure. But this is like looking for a needle in a haystack.'

Tim looked down at his father's face, illuminated by the yellow lantern light. ''Tisn't for that,' he said. 'I mean, not just for that. It's because you don't believe me.'

Mr Hoggart caught his breath. 'That's not true, Tim.'

'It *is*. I heard you this morning, talking to Mum. You don't believe about the cave or about what Mr Jones said or about the jewels . . . or . . . *anything*. You never do listen to me, you think I make things up all the time. That's why we came to the cave in the first place because the ruby'd been stolen, and I knew you'd never believe me . . .'

Mr Hoggart said slowly, 'I'm sorry, Tim. Sorry you couldn't trust me, I mean. That's my fault. I suppose I'm a dull and unimaginative man and so I always think explanations have to be dull and ordinary.' He looked at Tim and then smiled, suddenly. 'But you do make things up sometimes. You made up what I said to your mother, didn't you? I told her I believed you, but there was nothing we could do about it – or should. That it was up to the police, though I doubt whether they would do anything either. Not on your unsupported word. You see . . .'

'*You* believe me, though?' Tim interrupted him. Quite suddenly, it was all he cared about.

Mr Hoggart looked at him gravely. 'Yes, Tim, I do.' He hesitated. 'Do you believe *me*?'

Tim slid down from the boulder he was standing on, and put his hand in his father's. 'Yes, Dad,' he said. 'Shall we go and have lunch now?'

Janey was sitting in the mouth of the cave, examining a

sheep skull. 'This one's broken,' she complained. 'A bit of the jaw's gone. I don't want a nasty broken skull in my collection.'

'Wouldn't you rather collect something nice, dear?' her mother said. 'There must be lots of pretty shells on this beach.'

Janey scowled. 'I don't want to collect shells. I want to collect skulls. They're more useful.'

Mrs Hoggart made a resigned face and Tim grinned at her, feeling very grown up and cheerful. He went back into the cave. There were a good many skulls, washed up against the rocks, but it was harder than he expected to find a perfect one. Mr Tarbutt joined him. Between them they found several good skulls and dropped them beside Janey.

'Pick the best, I should,' Mr Tarbutt said.

'Not until after lunch, dear.' Mrs Hoggart was unpacking the picnic basket. 'Ham or chicken?'

Tim passed round the sandwiches, keeping one of each for himself. Janey took one bite and put her sandwich down. Her little hands stroked the skull lovingly. 'This one's a beauty,' she said. 'It's perfect, no nasty jagged edges.'

'Came off a shelf high up,' Mr Tarbutt said, casually glancing. 'The ones on the ground get damaged by the tide.'

'There's something inside it,' Janey said.

Her mother sighed. '*Do* put the nasty thing down while you're eating.'

She spoke without looking at Janey because she didn't want to make a fuss if the child disobeyed her. Mr Hoggart, who thought skulls were gruesome but perfectly hygienic, said nothing. He was busy opening a can of beer. Tim, stuffing the last of his second sandwich into his mouth, eyed the picnic basket and reckoned up how many more he was likely to get. Mr Tarbutt, stretched out lazily on the shingle, was munching slowly and watching the sea.

'Someone's been collecting stones,' Janey said.

They turned to look at her at last. She sat, her legs straight out in front of her, emptying the contents of a small leather bag into her lap.

No one spoke. No one had breath to speak. The little girl picked up the jewels and trickled them through her fingers. The sunlight caught them and seemed to set them on fire. Janey laughed.

'They feel like pretty stones,' she said. 'Are they pretty, Tim?'

17

A BUNCH OF FLOWERS FOR JANEY

PERDITA sat on the great rock in the bay. The gulls mewed round its battlements, diving, or just lazily drifting on the wind. She took no notice of them. She was staring out to sea. The steamer would be here soon. It would cross the bay and round the point into the harbour at Skuaphort and take Tim and Janey away.

She knew they were leaving. Annie had told her this morning when she had given her the presents they had sent up for her in Mr Duncan's van: a scarlet jersey from Janey – a new one she had never worn – and a necklace of beads from Tim. They were cheap green glass beads from Mr Duncan's store, and Perdita thought they were beautiful. She wore them now, over the scarlet jersey, and from time to time she touched them to make sure they were still there. They comforted her, but could not take away the ache in her heart.

Only one thing could do that, and she hadn't the courage for it. Though Mr Duncan had offered to take her down to the town to say good-bye to the children, she had shaken her head and clung to Annie. 'It's no good, she's still grieving,' Annie had said.

Grief was part of it, of course, but not all. Her own narrow escape from drowning had mercifully dulled her mind: by the time she had recovered from the shock and the physical exhaustion, the horror of that dreadful night seemed almost like a dream. Though she mourned for Mr Smith, it was with a gentle, blunted sadness, as for something that had happened a long time ago.

Tim and Janey were more real to her just now. When Mr Duncan had gone, she had rested in Annie's arms a minute, her face pressed into the old woman's shoulder. Then, as soon as she heard the van start up, she had torn herself away and run out of the house to call after him.

'Mr Duncan, Mr Duncan, wait for me . . .'

But the van was already jolting down the rutted road and he did not hear her. She had stood in the yard gate, the tears streaming down her face, until Annie had come out after her. 'Walk down to the hotel then, there's plenty of time,' she had said, but the only answer was a fresh outburst of painful tears and Annie had lost patience with her.

'Well – either you go or you don't, it's all one to me. I don't understand you, lady.'

Perdita did not understand herself. She felt as she had felt about the picnic yesterday: both longing and fearing, to go. It was part ordinary shyness, perhaps, part fear of Tim's questioning, part the hurtful memory of the way he had bullied her at the hotel – oh, so many things rolled up into one that it was impossible to sort them out. All she knew was this feeling which was a kind of trembly wanting and not-wanting, which grew more difficult to resolve with every passing minute. So she had put on her sweater and glass beads and come to the rock to comfort her sad heart.

But there was no comfort on the rock. She could not even shut her eyes and fly with the gulls in the air, because Tim had shown her that being a witch and flying and seeing round corners, was only a game she had played. She wasn't a witch any longer. She was only a lonely little girl. She had been lonely before, but she had never, in all her life, been lonely the way she was now. There would be other children to play with as soon as she went to school, Annie had told her, none of them would run away from her now, but at this moment she didn't want other children. She only wanted Tim and Janey – especially Janey. If she could only see her once more, say good-bye and hear her say she would come back one day, it would be all right . . .

She sat, irresolute and miserable, watching the sea. It was choppy today, flecked with white as far as the horizon, and the gulls on the surface of the water rocked, sideways on, to the waves. There was no sign of the steamer yet, but while she sat there, several small boats rounded the point and crossed the bay to the further headland. Perdita knew they were going to Carlin's Cave.

The news of Janey's discovery was all over the island, Mr Duncan had told Annie this morning. 'Up on a ledge, tucked inside a sheep skull – the cheek of it!' Mr Duncan had said. 'Staring you in the face, you might say. Thousands and thousands of pounds of rubies and diamonds and emeralds . . .'

In spite of this generous estimate, no one knew yet how large a part of the stolen jewels had been recovered, nor would they know, Mr Duncan had said, until the contents of Janey's little bag had been counted and checked. In the meantime, the police were trying hard to find Mr Campbell, a well-equipped salvage boat had come out from the mainland to investigate the sunken *Asti*, and almost everyone who could spare the time – and a good many who couldn't – were making their way by boat or on foot to Carlin's Cave. 'There won't be a skull left unturned on the island,' Mr Duncan had said, and laughed loudly at his own joke.

Perdita had heard all this without much interest, but now a new thought came into her mind. If most of the islanders were at the cave, there would be hardly anyone on the jetty to meet the steamer. Only the few who had to be there, and they would be too busy to bother about her, too busy to point at her and whisper behind their hands. It was one of the things she had feared most, she suddenly realized – that gauntlet of curious eyes!

She drew a deep breath and got to her feet. As she did so, the steamer came into view. The colour came up into her face. She was still shy, still frightened, but if she hesitated too long it would be too late. She gasped suddenly and turned to run but after a few steps she stopped abruptly, as if she had come up against a wall.

They had sent her presents. What could she give *them*? There was nothing – she had nothing of her own. Then she remembered that first day on the beach when she had found the sliver of rock with the leaf pressed into it. Janey had been pleased with that. But surely, real flowers would be better? She knew where some pretty ones grew, on a boggy patch beside a little stream: she had picked them sometimes for Annie. But *which* stream? As she looked wildly round her, the great rock seemed suddenly strange to her, like a foreign land. When she found the flowers at last, the breath was sobbing in her throat and her fingers were trembling so she could hardly pick them. She pulled them up in clumps – as many as she could, as many as she could hold. She stood upright and saw the steamer moving across the bay. It was nearly at the point.

Gasping, she went down off the rock and ran across the sand and up through the dunes. She cut her knee getting over the dry-stone wall and the warm blood trickled down her leg into her boot as she stumbled through the wet bog. When she reached the top of the ridge, the steamer was in the harbour and she stood for a minute, watching it with despairing eyes. The blood pounded in her head and the air was like a sword in her throat. Her mouth was dry. She licked her lips and began to run down the ridge. Her legs felt soft and shaky beneath her and the sky and the hillside seemed to jolt up and down in front of her eyes. She hadn't the strength to jump the stream by the ruined cottage and stumbled through it, slipping on the slimy pebbles so that she fell on the spongy ground of the opposite bank, flat on her face, crushing the flowers.

She lay there, spent. She had no more will, no more strength. It would be pleasant to lie there for ever, her feet in the cool, running stream, and her face on the earth. A kind of lovely sleepiness seemed to be stealing over her, a delicious peace. . . . She had to fight with herself – *against* herself – to get up, forcing one leg to move, then the other. Her legs felt queer as if they might easily bend backwards as well as forwards, and her head was singing.

She reached the stone road and thudded downhill. Her feet seemed to move by themselves, bang, *bang*, on the stone road, one, two, one, two. . . . She came into the town, rounded the corner by the school-house wall, and saw the jetty. There were very few people there. The mail van, Mr Duncan, Mr and Mrs Tarbutt. With a shock, she saw Mrs Tarbutt was waving.

Waving good-bye.

'Janey,' she sobbed inside her. 'Janey . . .'

She reached the jetty. She was too late. They were unfastening the gangplank and a man was unwinding a rope from one of the bollards. She looked up at the steamer through a mist of tears.

Janey and Tim were on deck, waving to Mrs Tarbutt. They did not see her. 'Wait, oh wait . . .' she tried to cry, 'look at me, I'm here . . .' but the words came out through her parched throat in a dry whisper. They were going and they had not seen her. The world blurred and shook in front of her eyes.

'Wait – wait – oh please, wait . . .'

For a moment, she was confused. That wasn't her, shouting. She couldn't shout. Nor could she rub her eyes with her hands because her hands were full of flowers. So she blinked and shook her head to shake the tears away and looked at the steamer.

It was Tim shouting. Red in the face, he had grabbed at the sailor who was removing the gangplank. He was jumping up and down.

Miraculously – at least, it seemed like a miracle to Perdita – someone took her by the arm. Mr Tarbutt said, 'You've been a long time. The little lass was grieving.'

She went, on wobbly legs, up the gangplank. 'I knew you'd come,' Janey said, at the top. 'They said you wouldn't, but I knew.'

'I picked you some flowers,' Perdita said, and thrust them into Janey's arms.

There was no time for more. There was no need for more. The ache in her heart was gone. She turned and walked down the gangplank and someone lifted her off on to the jetty.

'She brought me some flowers, Dad,' Janey said to her father.

'Did she? That was nice – she's waving, wave back, Janey.'

'I can't, holding all this stuff.'

'Give it to me, then.' Mr Hoggart took the flowers and Janey began to wave with both arms, like a windmill. He glanced down at the mass of flowers in his hands, and then looked more closely. He whistled softly under his breath. The delicate, purplish petals were crushed and damaged, no use as specimens, but they were quite unmistakable. They were the rare flowers, the 'black orchids' he had been looking for. 'Where did she get them, I wonder?' he said, speaking to himself, and then he laughed. 'Well – I've only to ask her,' he said answering his own question, and turned to his son. 'Tell her we'll be back,' he said. 'Soon. Soon as we can manage.'

'Good-bye – we'll come back,' Tim shouted...

'Soon,' Janey cried. 'We'll be back soon ...'

The little girl stood on the jetty and waved and the two children leaned over the rail of the steamer and waved too. The steamer drew away from the jetty and the dirty water pumped out of the bilges and the gulls wheeled round, crying and looking for titbits. The steamer moved out of the harbour and the jetty grew small and the people on it smaller too, until they were just dots of colour, and then not even dots, but nothing at all.

'There's no point in waving now,' Tim said to Janey, 'you can't see her any more.'

'I can in my mind, you stupid thing,' Janey said.

Another book by Nina Bawden in Puffin

THE RUNAWAY SUMMER

When Mary meets Simon, the policeman's son, on the beach she's in the mood to do something really dramatic. After all, life at home is impossible.

So when they discover the Kenyan boy who has been smuggled illegally into the country, it seems a good idea to help hide him on the island that Simon knows about, while Mary searches for his mysterious uncle in London.